"Set against the vibrant yet gritty backdrop of Los Angeles, these stories bring to life the inner worlds of characters who seek—and sometimes stumble upon—meaningful connections. Artists, writers, and everyday Angelenos alike face the thrilling, precarious dance of closeness and longing, each choice reverberating with humor, heartbreak, and revelation. Intelligent without pretense, *Daddy Issues* captures a nuanced portrait of LA's mosaic of lives on the edge of change, for anyone who has known the precarious business of intimacy."

—Steven Reigns, author of *A Quilt for David* and *Inheritance*

"Unstinting and deep, *Daddy Issues* roils the mirror surfaces of our days with cutting candor and intense, unexpected compassion. Eric Wat's characters body forth revelatory insight as they emerge from marginalization into hard fought light."

—Sesshu Foster, author of *Atomic Aztex*

"In *Daddy Issues* Eric C. Wat has written a collection of short stories as profound as they are humorous. In doing so, he deftly challenges conventions while illuminating the resilience of the human spirit. Wat's intricate storytelling and vivid prose offers us an unvarnished examination of love, loss, longing, and the ties that bind us to one another. An absolutely essential addition to contemporary literature."

—Alex Espinoza, author of *The Sons of El Rey*

"These stories capture, with insight, humor, and tenderness, what it feels like to have issues of various kinds, to look at oneself squarely and change. There are no heroes here (though perhaps an antihero or two). One walks into an Eric C. Wat story as if into a room where everyone is trying to stay alive, a room filled with quotidian surfaces and charged, transformational depths. Wat's multigenerational, cross-cultural stories explore the often tangled perils and pleasures of trust, vulnerability, silence, sacrifice, and love."

—Jennifer Tseng, author of *Mayumi and the Sea of Happiness* and *Thanks for Letting Us Know You Are Alive*

DADDY ISSUES

ZERO STREET FICTION

Series Editors
Timothy Schaffert
SJ Sindu

DADDY ISSUES

STORIES

ERIC C. WAT

University of Nebraska Press
Lincoln

The University of Nebraska Press is part of a land-grant institution with campuses and programs on the past, present, and future homelands of the Pawnee, Ponca, Otoe-Missouria, Omaha, Dakota, Lakota, Kaw, Cheyenne, and Arapaho Peoples, as well as those of the relocated Ho-Chunk, Sac and Fox, and Iowa Peoples.

For customers in the EU with safety/GPSR concerns, contact:
gpsr@mare-nostrum.co.uk
Mare Nostrum Group BV
Mauritskade 21D
1091 GC Amsterdam
The Netherlands

Library of Congress Cataloging-in-Publication Data

Names: Wat, Eric C., 1970- author.
Title: Daddy issues: stories / Eric C. Wat.
Other titles: Daddy issues (Compilation)
Description: Lincoln: University of Nebraska Press, 2025. |
Series: Zero Street fiction
Identifiers: LCCN 2024056858
ISBN 9781496243584 (paperback)
ISBN 9781496244161 (epub)
ISBN 9781496244178 (pdf)
Subjects: LCSH: Asian American sexual minorities—Fiction. | Asian Americans—Fiction. | BISAC: FICTION / Short Stories (single author) | FICTION / Asian American | LCGFT: Queer fiction. | Short stories.
Classification: LCC PS3573.A7985 D33 2025 |
DDC 813/.54—dc23/eng/20250314
LC record available at https://lccn.loc.gov/2024056858

Designed and set in Bulmer MT Std by Lacey Losh.

You become. It takes a long time. That's why it doesn't happen often to people who break easily, or have sharp edges, or who have to be carefully kept. Generally, by the time you are Real, most of your hair has been loved off, and your eyes drop out and you get loose in your joints and very shabby. But these things don't matter at all, because once you are Real you can't be ugly, except to people who don't understand.

The Velveteen Rabbit, Margery Williams

I want to be someone I've never been before.

Octavia E. Butler

CONTENTS

ACKNOWLEDGMENTS

A lot of us started with Short Stories. Short Stories was our first love. It was how we honed our craft. Short Stories had a lot to teach, and then we outgrew it. We set our sights on longer and (what we thought were) more mature relationships. Now and again, we came back to Short Stories, like when a Novel fizzled after a few chapters. Or even when a Novel succeeded—especially the kind that thought of itself as the Great American—after we shared it with the rest of the world, it no longer belonged to us. Every time we came back, Short Stories welcomed us with open arms. We found something new in our lovemaking, because we were different people now. Until the next Big Idea. Then Short Stories kissed our forehead and let us go.

If we have the fortune to be a writer of some longevity, this cycle happens over and over again. Without fail, we come home to Daddy.

I've kept all our love letters. Many of them, spanning over two decades, are in this collection. I wrote the earliest story here after my friends' miscarriage. Now my friends have a child about to enter college. A couple of stories were composed during the COVID-19 pandemic, when new affairs with the long form that held some promise in the beginning didn't pan out. Short Stories is special, especially when the love letters are not scattered in literary journals or anthologies but brought together in one place. I see myself more clearly, more completely, here than any one body of work. For this, I have the University of Nebraska Press to thank, especially the series editors of Zero Street Fiction, Timothy Schaffert and SJ Sindu. You know you've found the right publishers when your editors describe your book the way you want to be described as a person. Timothy in particular offered reassuring and constructive advice throughout the editorial process. I have read both their works before. That two novelists with such a beautiful command of language chose this collection for the Zero Street series still feels nothing short of a miracle to me sometimes. Also, I tip my hat to Courtney Ochsner (acquisition editor), Rebecca Jefferson (marketing associate), Abbey Frankforter (assistant project editor), Kerin Tate (copy-editor), and many others who worked behind the scene at UNP to bring this book to life. Perhaps like a masochist, I actually enjoy the copyediting process because I always learn something about the language. I didn't realize, after being in the U.S. for years, I had been using British spelling for some words, the way I learned it as a child in pre-handover Hong Kong. I guess you can take a boy out of the colony, but it is hard to take the colony out of the boy. At least in this respect, Kerin came pretty close.

As a short story writer, I am influenced by so many peers that I've had (and continue to have) the privilege of building a creative community with. Euphronia Awakuni, Lisa Hernandez, and Jennifer Tseng have read many of these stories in their earliest incarnations. But there are so many others: Noel Alumit, Anna Alves, Chi-Wai Au, Deanna Cherry, Maisie Chin, Julie Cho, Enji Chung, Dana Collins, Xiomara Corpeño, Myra Dumapias, Sesshu Foster, Gwen Gary-Ramsay, Julie Ha, Naomi Hirahara, Kelly Jeong, Nancy I. Kim, Sky Kogachi, Chen Lin, David Maruyama, Mike Murashige, Joyce Nako, Vy Nguyen, Amy Pabalan, Darlene Rodrigues, Mari Ryono, Saúl Sarabia, Irene Soriano Sexton, Liz Sunwoo, Brett Tam, joël b. tan, Allan Tijamo, Diep Tran, Chris Tucker, and Karen Yin. They have shared their works with me, given me feedback, organized readings and events with me, or just sat down quietly with me for a few hours in a morning so we could concentrate on our craft. They taught me the value of vulnerability in a writer and showed me that the profession didn't have to be a lonely one.

I have eternal gratitude for my brother Albert Y. Wat, who was my emotional anchor as I explored the dark that gave way to the stories in this collection. Writing can be uncomfortable and even scary, but Albert makes sure I can always come back home.

As I searched for the more remote recess in my mind to make sure I didn't forget anyone to thank (I probably still have), this memory came up. When I was in eighth grade, I was agonizing over the fact that English, my new everyday language, still intimidated me; I had only immigrated from Hong Kong a year before. My classmate Miles said, "What are you talking about? You already speak Chinese, and it's just a matter of time before you speak English like the rest of us. You're going to be bilingual. You know how special that makes you?" It's a marvel how one small thing that someone says can change the way you look at yourself years later and make your dream feel a little more plausible. You might not remember it all the time, but when you do, you realize how that small thing, along with other small kindnesses you've collected in your path, is already a part of you.

I won't forget the lovers, too. There are no stories without them, but they will remain unnamed.

DADDY ISSUES

THIS BUSINESS OF DEATH

Because it was Sunday dim sum rush hour, the restaurant put our post-funeral luncheon in the small room upstairs that was usually reserved for the bridal party at a wedding banquet. From the tail end, I saw our people snake through the crowd and din of the dining hall to reach the loft above: generations of noises, waiters hustling with sauces and clean plates, cart ladies hawking their steaming tins on any table where you could still see glass on the lazy Susan. Despite our somber look, we had to stand in wait for these cart ladies to complete their transactions. Finally, we passed the last waiter's station and then, one after the other, filed up the narrow staircase to our room. At the corner of the room was a bar without any liquor. The couch was pushed against the wall, along with the movable closet where the bride would hang her many changes of clothes. Empty hangers dangled from it. Carton boxes anchored it below. This had been my aunt's favorite Chinese restaurant in all of San Gabriel Valley when she was alive. They'd managed to arrange five tables in this loft; she would've considered it a good showing.

The cart ladies wouldn't come up. They didn't have to. On behalf of my cousins, I'd ordered the same set of dishes, eight in all, for every table ahead of time. By the time the soup came, the room was as rowdy as the scene below us. The rest of the dishes came fast and furious, and the eaters devoured them in the same fashion. In another ten minutes, the salt-and-pepper pork chops was just a plate of bones. After dessert (a watered-down red bean paste, pretty much a soup), some guests began to stand up and visit with each other. The waiters brought a stack of Styrofoam boxes to each table for the leftovers.

The host table included the three surviving children, my cousins Ben, Clark, and Eliza (in that birth order); Clark's wife, Zara, and their two teenage children, twins; and our two uncles, bachelors who had outlived the last woman in their generation. There had been some debate, and in the end Eliza's boyfriend, Xander, was also invited to that table. When it looked like people wanted to leave, Clark stood up. Eliza followed, and then Ben. They lined up by the door to say thanks and goodbye. I was pretty sure you only did that at weddings. This might be the most matrimonial vestige in the room.

Eliza was collecting envelopes from the departing guests. The way she was clutching them, I could tell she was feeling their heft. My eight-year-old son Jeremy looked up between levels of Angry Birds on his iPad and asked me what was in those envelopes. I only had him every other weekend. This was not supposed to be my weekend, but the ex made a rare exception for funerals.

I said it was money.

"Like birthdays?" Jeremy asked.

"Kind of."

When I had told him about his great-aunt's death, he took it matter-of-factly, as far as I could tell over the phone. I had a feeling that my ex had already talked to him about it, not trusting me to handle a delicate subject like death with a boy his age. She had a knack about talking to children like they were adults. I was loath to admit that the philosophy came in handy this time. I was off the hook. My vague answer about the envelopes puzzled him more, though not enough to keep him from his game. I let this one go, too, thinking this was not the kind of tradition he would have to worry about.

I looked up at Clark and saw that my aunt's mahjong friends began to queue up. In the spectrum of guests, I was an in-between, closer to the hosts than other guests but not enough to sit at the head table. I couldn't leave before other guests, but I wasn't expected to stay behind to settle the check. While I waited, Clark's wife, Zara, came to my table and scooted next to me.

"Hey, Jer," Zara said to my son on my other side.

From his iPad, Jeremy looked up at her to confirm the voice's identity. He did this a lot, at least with people on my side. Sometimes I thought he could tell his mother's friends by their voices without looking up. He looked at her for three full seconds before he finally said, "Hi, Aunt Zara."

She moved in closer, like she wanted to see his game. I could see the dark crown of her head, silky strands straightened and cascading down. "You look taller than the last time I saw you."

"How would you know? I'm sitting down."

"Jeremy!" I shouted at him and put my hand on the screen, fingers spreading and covering as much of it as possible. I knew why he said it. He had missed a trick because she broke his concentration. Jeremy had always been a "sensitive" child, as the ex would say. She said "sensitive" like it was a virtue that needed to be encouraged, but Jeremy was not sensitive like empathetic, just easily hurt or irritated. He used to cry readily when life wasn't turning out as he'd expected; now, he acted out against people with what the ex thought was wit. *A wuss with a smart mouth will get himself in a lot of trouble.* It was not the kind of thing that a father should think or say (though I had done both). "Apologize to your aunt," I said.

"I'm sorry." He wasn't disingenuous about it. At least he still listened to a stern voice.

"It's all right. We're all a little on edge these days." She reached over and roughed up his hair a little.

Jeremy was smart enough to let her, but he still rubbed one in when he turned to me and protested, "But I'm NOT growing taller."

"Be patient, kid. You will soon." For all our sakes, I acted like it was a complaint, not truth-telling. I sensed by now that Zara hadn't come to my table for company. So I sent my son away. "Go play with your cousins."

Head down and iPad in both hands, Jeremy went between Zara's twins, as if he were passing through two redwoods.

I told Zara, "Now your sons. Look at them. They're much taller than I thought anyone in our family could be. Must be your genes."

The boys always had dark eyes like their mother's. When Clark and Zara were dating, she told me that her mother taught her how to put on eye makeup, and nobody knew how to do that better than Arabic women because for centuries eyes were all they could show to the world. Her sons always reminded me of that conversation. The boys had lashes thicker than any of the young men in my school, or many young women, for that matter. Zara usually grew soft when people complimented her children. When I turned to her, I was surprised to find her brows furrowed, making her own eyelashes fan in a beautiful way, delicate by their length and intimidating by their precision.

"Clark told me what happened," she began hesitantly, "when you were young."

"What do you mean?"

"I don't know why I'm telling you this. I don't know what I want by having this conversation. It's just that . . ."

"Spit it out, Zara. What is it?"

"Clark said," she closed her eyes and opened them again as if she had found the words in the dark. Smoky. I had had no idea what people meant when they described eyes like that—how do eyes smoke?—until I met Zara. "He said you two *explored* each other when you were teenagers."

I was shocked. Frankly, I had forgotten about it. That shocked me more than the fact that she was talking to me about it now. And *explored*? That was the word that was summoned in her third eye?

She continued, "Maybe we shouldn't be having this conversation here. But we don't see you much anymore, except this business of death." She twirled her hand, acknowledging the room. "You've been so helpful, Walter, and I don't want you to think there was anything wrong with what you guys did. I know it happens to more people than most of us think. There is no shame." She paused. "I don't know what I want from this."

I wasn't going to bail her out or fill her silence. I concentrated on the collection of sauce dishes in front of me, swirled combinations of gravy, soy sauce, and chili paste drowning twigs of fried noodles and half-melted ice cubes—work of my young son, another cultural transgression, but a battle also not picked this time. It would all be a big mess if the waiters were not careful. *Where are the waiters? Why do I have to think of everything for everyone?*

Finally, I said, "Jesus, Zara. That was so long ago."

"I know. And I know Clark's not into men."

The irony is, if I were not into men either, if I had not come out, this wouldn't have been an issue.

She continued, "I don't know what I want. I don't want it to threaten me, but maybe it does. It's not like you two have done anything since or will do anything like that again. I'm not fishing. I know he's not into men."

"You said that."

"I did. How can we talk so calmly about this?"

"When did Clark tell you this?"

"He told his mother the day before she died. She was lying there unconscious and he was just blurting out all kinds of stuff like it was confession. And this came out. I was right there. He asked me afterward if I thought she could hear him."

"Do you think she could?"

Zara gave me a look that told me it was a stupid question. It was the same look I told my new teachers to never give to their students. "He asked if I would forgive him, too. I don't know why he asked me. When there's really nothing to forgive. Right? You guys just touched each other. He wouldn't say anything when I asked for more. What could I do? He was grieving. I said, 'Of course.' He wouldn't talk about it since. So you see, Walter, I know practically nothing."

She stopped. She now expected reciprocation. She *was* fishing. I realized then that the words "forget" and "remember" could not cover all the experiences of our memories. I had not really forgotten. Age might have put some things away, but it was coming back to me now. It wasn't the kind of thing you'd forget.

"Zara, I was twelve when I moved in with them. Clark was thirteen. We shared the same room. My aunt was pretty much a divorcée, a single mother, working full time and taking care of not only her kids, but also me and my mom, who was in her room most of the time. We were teenagers left alone all the time, with not much to do. There were no . . . iPads." I delivered this in my officious tone, the one that my therapist said I used to appear calm, the one I honed perfectly as a vice-principal in dealing with pesky students and their parents, but with which, in private matters, I intended to forestall intimacy. Like this room, hollowed temporarily for another purpose. I continued, "We were curious. Like all teenagers were."

She looked at me, expecting more. I know what she wanted to ask, but I wasn't going to offer whether I'd known I was gay then. That would explain everything to her and nothing to me. I stared right back at her, unrelenting. She blinked first, with those big eyes, and then I looked away at the remaining cast of characters. Neither one of us was quite a part of this. Before her sons came along, we'd been closer because of this. There was usually just one dinner table then, none of this fanfare, and Zara and I would sneak out before dessert for a smoke and gossip about them. When they drove her crazy, I was the one she sought advice from. More than understanding this family, I knew how to manage them.

For old times' sake, I added, "It was just grief talking."

To this, Zara blankly said, "It was that, too."

My aunt died of septic shock after she was admitted to the hospital for pneumonia in the right lung, a complication of her high blood pressure, spiking just three days before. She was seventy-nine. It was her fourth hospital stay in five years. She had a stroke a week before her seventy-fifth birthday. The second time was after she fractured her hip when she slipped down the last three steps of the stairs at home. The third time was also pneumonia. Each time she came out, she was much worse than before, as if she left a little of herself behind in those sterile rooms. First, her memory went. Then her legs gave out, and her fingers wouldn't close around a pair of chopsticks, and only a few weeks later, not even a fork or a spoon.

After the third hospital stay, Eliza and her boyfriend, Xander, moved in. Eliza was seven years younger than Clark and twelve years apart from Ben, the eldest. I had always suspected that the distance between the siblings' births was a sign of ongoing tumult in the marriage between my aunt and uncle, who was coming in and out of her life. When Eliza moved in, she insisted that she be put down as the next of kin. No one was going to fight her for it, but she still went about it aggressively, sounding as if her mother's hospitalization was the sole result of neglect by everyone but her.

I only knew this because Zara told me, and she only told me because she knew it was a not-so-veiled accusation directed at her. Ben was a bachelor and had moved away since college. Clark had plenty of love for my aunt, but like all favorite sons, he never had to do much to earn it; nor was he expected to. I had no doubt Zara's hunch was right, but I saw no point in adding fuel to fire if I had to be the one to put it out eventually. So I told Zara that when Eliza was a child, her mom was taking care of everyone else, so she was a little possessive. It was a cop-out but not a complete lie. Eliza was never the baby of the family. By the time she was old enough to figure out that adults could have favorites, her father was gone and her mother spent what remained of her energy every day to make sure her sister, my mom, knew that she was loved.

Only after I'd pinned the source of Eliza's problem on my dead mother did my betrayal gall me into admitting what a peacemaker in this family I'd become.

Zara was satisfied, if begrudgingly. "Your cousin might have never felt she was the center of anyone's universe when she was a child, but she's more than making up for it now."

I had no problem conceding that to put an end to that conversation.

Eliza was nowhere near the caregiver that her mother was, even after she'd had some practice coddling many a freeloading boyfriend since college. Xander, the current one, was supposed to take care of my aunt while Eliza slaved for the city as a structural engineer. All he had to do was heat up the meals that Eliza had prepared for her mother and remind her to take her meds. She had one TV and he monopolized it. Half the time the old woman hid in her room. My aunt had told me all this in the first day of her hospital stay. She had told me, and me alone, because she'd expected me to do something about that.

But she never left that hospital room again. She died six days after she was admitted, at 2:30 in the morning. Eliza got the call first, and she called Clark, Ben, and me, in that order. But I was the first to arrive, not even half an hour after the time of death. Clark and Zara came next. By then, they'd removed her dentures, and her lips caved into her mouth. Her skin, no longer replenished from the IV, fell loosely around her bones. Her veins were more blue than I'd remembered.

Eliza came almost two hours after the call, with Xander in tow. She made the nurse retell the last hours of her mother's life—her stats the last time the nurse checked, what she ate and did not eat of her dinner, how hard she was breathing through the respirator, what time her doctor was called when they knew she wasn't going to make it. As the details were rehashed, Clark and Eliza left the room. Only I remained, mesmerized by the blank heart rate monitor. How strange it looked without data or noise, as if it had died with her. I looked at the body, and back at the monitor, and then the body again, unsure which was the cause and which its effect.

Eliza started crying about how no one came to see her mother that day, and how her mother had died alone on the one day she had to work twelve hours. When I held her, she repeated this, only louder, especially the twelve-hour bit. She cried louder to get Clark and Zara back into the room. When they did, she screamed, "I can't do this. I can't do this by myself anymore," as if there was much left to do. Two more nurses came in from their station to tell her to calm down. Eliza broke away from me and pounded on Clark's chest as she wailed. He held her by the back of her head, her hair spilling between his fingers. He was a head taller than her. Clark was crying, too. His chest absorbed her sound, and her hair muffled his.

I had visited my aunt that afternoon, like I had every afternoon, after school. I was there to read to her. I didn't say anything because I didn't want to take away Eliza's moment. I wasn't supposed to care more about her mother than she. I was sick of this sorry sight. I grazed past Zara, walked around the floor, and ran into Xander. He was texting someone on his fancy phone.

Eliza had bereavement leave but didn't have time to take it. Clark fell ill (from grief, said Zara). And that being the beginning of the twins' junior year, they had too many after-school commitments readying for college, and they were not old enough to drive themselves. Eliza thought Zara was useless, anyway, and said as much to everyone but her. She had the illusion that Xander was the closest to her mother in her dying days and that he could be Eliza's proxy at the funeral home. Ben called from where he lived in Kansas. He wasn't planning to come to LA until much closer to the funeral and he asked me to intervene. So I did.

Eliza told me that Xander didn't need help. I had no choice but to tell her that her eldest brother disagreed.

"It's not fair that no one has ever considered Xander part of the family. I don't know why Ben is sticking his nose in this. I've talked to the funeral director, and everything is settled. I just need someone to go over the details."

In my most detached voice, I tried to please both sides. "It doesn't hurt to have a second person there, but if you don't think it's necessary, I won't go."

I could hear her talking to someone else on the other end. Then she came back. "If you could give Xander a ride, that would be great. His car has been in the shop for almost a week now, and he still doesn't know when he'll be getting it back."

As always, Eliza overestimated her ability: Not much had been settled with the funeral director. The coffin that she had picked out was more expensive than she thought. (I covered the difference.) The director wanted the clothes that my aunt would be buried in, but Xander swore he knew nothing about it. Neither did he have my aunt's Chinese name written on a piece of paper that Eliza promised for the engraving on the headstone. (Fortunately, I knew that by heart.) The photo of my aunt Eliza had sent for the program was "too young," said the director. We tried to reach Eliza, but every call went straight to voicemail. Decisions were contingent on other decisions not made. Each uncertainty multiplied itself. Halfway through the meeting, as I was writing down yet another question I couldn't answer, Xander walked out and said he would text her.

He never came back. After the meeting, I found him in my car, windows rolled down. His feet were on my dashboard. He was whispering on the phone but cackling loudly. When he saw me, he put his feet down and turned away from me. Xander reminded me of those students I'd catch smoking pot in their cars in the school's parking lot, except they were less obvious.

"Was that Eliza?" I ran toward my car. "Why did you hang up? You know we've been trying to get a hold of her."

"She had to go." He looked up at me from his seat, squinting his eyes like my head was the sun. "She said if you have any questions, I can ask her for you."

I decided that getting to the bottom of his lie would be as futile as busting teenagers getting high in cars that were worth almost my annual salary. I tore the page off my notebook. "These are not *my* questions."

The funeral had to be postponed another week because Eliza didn't get back to the funeral director on time. The delay pissed off Ben, who'd booked his plane ticket for that weekend already. He called me because he couldn't get a straight answer from his siblings. "I thought you'd take care of everything," he said, but then quickly had the sense to add it wasn't my responsibility, close enough of an apology. He asked whether he should pay $150 to change his ticket at the last minute, and then he answered himself that a mother's funeral was probably a good enough excuse to waive the fee.

"Or you could just come this weekend."

"For what?" Ben went on to complain about how Clark and Eliza could not plan anything. Clark, because he always did what he wanted and their mother let him. Eliza? He mumbled something but couldn't settle on one reason for her incompetence. I hate people who complain about others not doing things right when they do not lift a finger themselves; I hate them more than incompetent people. Ben hadn't even been there in my aunt's last days. He just made us put the phone to his mother's ear, while he screamed, loud enough above the respirator, as he prayed to God with her that He would deliver her from the latest mishap.

"Maybe they need you."

"Who are we kidding?" Ben said. "My mother always resented me for not coming home after college, just like my father never came back. She always thought we were the same." He choked up a little when he said this. I thought about my sensitive boy and sighed quietly on my end. Who keeps decades-old grudges in their head? After college? Really? I mustered enough sympathy to tell Ben I was sorry for his loss.

The weekend after the funeral, Eliza asked me to help her clean out her mother's room. I asked where Xander was. She said he needed a vacation. Now that her mother was gone, Eliza thought he deserved a break. She even paid for the trip to Cabo. After all, she justified, Xander had saved them a lot of money by not having to hire a home health worker. I thought her too much of an idiot to deny her request. Besides, part of me wanted to do this. My aunt had pictures of us that I wanted for myself.

After Eliza let me in, I found a note by the credenza in the living room and thought it looked familiar. It had all the questions I'd jotted down for Eliza just a few weeks before, except the paper and the handwriting were different. The bastard had copied it and passed it along as his own. Eliza saw me read the list. She said, "Wasn't Xander wonderful? Just when I thought he wasn't paying attention, he was more helpful to me than I'd even hoped for."

"I think we should start."

I found the photo albums inside my aunt's closet. She had eight, all the same kind. I took the pictures out of their plastic sleeves. Selfishly I picked out the ones I wanted and put them in one pile, and separated the others arbitrarily into three other piles, one for each sibling. The last album was mostly black-and-whites, and it had many pictures of my aunt and my mother in their youth. In some, I couldn't tell them apart. I waved at Eliza from across the room. I pointed at the album and asked, "Can I just keep this one? It has a lot of pictures of my mom." As I expected, Eliza nodded indifferently.

There were two boxes in the upper reaches of the closet. I remembered them because I had hoisted them there. These were my aunt's old books, mostly romance novels from a prolific Taiwanese writer and a few martial arts epics. She'd loaned them to me when I was in college, eighty paperbacks and all. I'd been taking Chinese classes. She was very proud of me for that. I'd transferred two or three books at a time from her room to my dorm, until I had her entire collection. When I separated from my ex and moved to a smaller apartment, I returned them to her in these same boxes.

Next to the boxes was a small open box with rings of water spots and a faded UPS label. I pulled it down. It was lighter than I thought, and all its contents came tumbling out. A dozen pill bottles, half of them opaque, all nearly empty. Together, they made a hollow rattling noise as they fell. I knew right away what they were: decongestants, antidepressants, calcium supplements, stool softeners, estrogen hormones, painkillers. They were my mother's. I recognized the Ativan by their shapes. I used to think they looked like tiny houses. Someone had told me that my mother would feel better once she took these hexagon pills because she was swallowing love. What she couldn't feel from me in her heart, she could ingest in the shape of our home. Instead, she'd taken more and more drugs, using one to counter the side effects of another.

What she couldn't feel from me in her heart, she could ingest in the shape of our home. Holding the bottle, I thought, *Who would say something like this to a child?* Then I remembered I'd told Jeremy not too long ago that his great-aunt passed away because she worked so hard all her life and was so filled with love for all of us for so long that her heart burst. I thought, *Is this the lesson we pass on: love, too much or not enough, causes death?*

The night after my mother killed herself, I crawled into bed with Clark. We cuddled. He didn't rub himself against me like he usually did. Although we were about the same age, he had experienced a growth spurt a few months earlier than I. And when we wrapped around each other, my forehead could touch his chin. For the first time, he kissed me, first on my eye, then my nose, and finally flat on my lips, each a permission for what followed. It was kind. It was not a playful experiment. He did it like he knew it was what you were supposed to do to make someone feel better. A month later, when Ben moved away to college, Clark could've moved into his room, but he didn't. He stayed with me. That was kind, too.

This was what I had not remembered but could not forget.

I didn't know why my aunt kept these pill bottles with the old photographs and dusty books. When I gathered them, I sobbed quietly. Something surged in my throat, wide, bitter-acidic, and unwieldy, perhaps like the shape of a house. I pushed it down. I didn't know if I was crying for my mother or my aunt, but it was the first time I had cried since my aunt's passing. When I knew I could no longer sob without Eliza noticing, I dropped the bottles on the floor and rushed out of the room.

In the bathroom, I called Clark on my phone. He picked up only after one ring.

"Walter?"

"Clark."

When I didn't say more, he asked, "What is it, Walter?" After some silence, he repeated, "What is it, Walter? You can't call me like this."

Tell me, Clark. Say the right thing, please, I thought to myself.

We both didn't speak. How sad, I thought then, that for the one thing I wanted to hear someone tell me, I had no one to ask except Clark.

At my retreat, he confronted me, "What did you say to Zara? I saw you two talking at the restaurant. What did you tell her?" He didn't let me answer before he pressed on, "I won't have this over us. What did you tell her?"

Because he wouldn't say it, because no one else would, I screamed, "She was my mother, too!"

Nobody, not even the doctors, knew whether my aunt could hear us in her last days. My cousins were convinced of it, but it was wishful thinking. Ben prayed with her, long-distance, to get better. Eliza told her that Xander would keep the house clean for her return. Clark cried inconsolably each time he left her room. I read to her every afternoon when no one was there. That afternoon before she passed, I leaned in and kissed her cheek to say goodbye. Her skin was cold, wrinkly but soft. I told her, "If you want to go, Aunt, you should go. Your children are all fine. I'm good, too. I will look out for them, like you looked out for my mother and me." I had meant it when I said it. I held her face as if that could help her hear my words better.

When she passed later, I thought maybe she had.

But when I left Eliza that day, without an explanation and empty-handed, I knew I was not up to the task.

My ex and I had decided a few years ago that neither of us would tell Jeremy that the reason we separated was because I had come out of the closet. Jeremy wasn't even five at the time. I told my ex before I told Clark and Eliza. I said Clark could tell Zara and it was up to them whether they would tell the twins. I'd prefer them not to, because I didn't want Jeremy's cousins to know before he did. I said Eliza could tell Ben but not the boyfriend she was dating at the time. And no one could tell my aunt except me.

It took me another two years to come out to her, after her first bout with pneumonia. She said she was okay with it. But then after she came out of the hospital, whether out of denial or early onset of dementia, or just plain cleverness in taking advantage of her forgetfulness, she continued to pester me with questions about how I planned to reunite with my ex. I always shrugged, like I had a plan not ready to be revealed, but inside I was convinced that, even if I had corrected her, she would forget it eventually.

My ex wanted to be honest with Jeremy as soon as possible, but I reminded her that it was my decision to make. I told her that I was putting a lot of trust in her by sharing my secret, knowing that she could use it against me to keep me away from Jeremy.

She said, "First of all, I don't think that would work in most courts nowadays. And second, I'm offended that you think so little of me." I tried not to make too much about the fact that her "second" wasn't her "first of all." In the end, she still got Jeremy almost all of the time when they moved away to Riverside.

Recently, she told me that it was getting difficult to get Jeremy excited about coming to see me on the appointed weekend, even though he was staying with me only every other week. She said that Jeremy told his therapist that I was too structured, that I was withholding. I didn't doubt that she was telling the truth, though I hoped those were not the exact words that Jeremy used. I asked myself, *How could you be a father to someone four days out of the month?* Because I couldn't say that, I reacted with humor. The ex wasn't amused. I had told my own therapist that every time Jeremy uttered the word *water*, I had a nagging fear that my son was calling me by my first name. I might score some points with my ex by being this vulnerable, but I found myself not caring. Score one for *my* therapist.

On a Sunday afternoon, in our last hours together, Jeremy and I watched a Lakers game on TV. It was the first round of the playoffs. We each sat on a beanbag, one yellow and the other green. It was the kind that my aunt used to have in their house. Clark and I would sit like ship captains on them and play his Atari, blasting aliens or dodging ghosts with joysticks. My uncle, when he was around, would pull his beanbag up close to the TV (before the time of remote control) so he could change the channels without ever getting up. He leaned into the beanbag like a propped-up pillow rather than a seat. Clark and I would stay up and watch Johnny Carson with him, while upstairs my aunt slept with my mother. During the summer nights, my uncle would be shirtless, and Clark would unbutton his pajama top. Sitting sideways, one half of the shirt would dangle, exposing half his chest. Coyly I copied him, but neither had the guts to remove our tops completely like my uncle. We just looked at each other and sometimes giggled nervously. When I became a father and Jeremy was just learning how to walk, I had bought two beanbags on the kind of whim that my ex still found intoxicating in those days. After the separation, she asked me to vacate them from her house.

To be less withholding, earlier that morning, I'd let Jeremy have coffee with a lot of cream and play with his iPad for over an hour before I tore it away. To my son's credit, while showing little interest in the basketball game on TV, he sat still in the yellow beanbag reading my old copy of *Watership Down*.

Kobe Bryant had just made one of his trademark fade-away shots with less than a second on the shot clock and two people in his face. "Jeremy, did you see what Kobe did?" I asked, knowing full well that he had not. I wanted a conversation.

Jeremy looked up from the book, canting his head to let me know that he was being interrupted. "Mom said Kobe Bryant is a rapist." He wanted a reaction. He took after his mother. He was smart, maybe too much for his own good.

I didn't want to give him one. So I just said, "Fair enough."

"I think I can say *rapist*. I know what it means."

"You know. Someone can be a rapist and still be great at something." It was an entirely idiotic thing to say to a child, no matter how true. Why was I talking to him like he was his mother? I couldn't wait to see how this was going to boomerang back to me.

"Mom watches tennis." That was new, but not unexpected.

"Tennis is good, too. I think there is a lot of grace and beauty in athletics . . . in any sports."

"I know what athletics means. What I don't know, Dad . . ." I was pleased to hear him say the word *Dad*, but he stressed it a little too ironically. With other children, I could push it off as unintentional. ". . . is why when someone has zero points in tennis, they call it love."

"Let's look it up." I turned on the iPad, whose battery was drained down to its last 5 percent. I started typing, *tennis score love*. Right when I was about to hit *search*, Jeremy said, "I have another question, Dad." A much softer call this time.

"What is it?"

"What if I want to marry a boy?"

I looked at him. Jeremy's expression was playful, not a drop of malice. The trace of his mother was gone. Instead, he reminded me of my own mother, of those bright moments before she fell into depression. In those moments, she'd been as guileless as my son was now, and then she broke my heart. I looked away and kept my head down, pretending to wait for the page to load. I took a deep breath and sorted out my thoughts. This was going to be the time. There would be no better time. I saw the answers to his first question filling up the screen. By then I already honed in on his last, making up my mind that I would tell him the truth, that it would be okay, that I, more than anyone else my son would know, would understand and love him no matter who he was. What could I say to lasso him and hold on to him a little longer? I only stared at him blankly.

To fill my silence, or to make me forget what he'd asked, Jeremy rehashed an old question: "Why did they give Aunt Eliza money when great-aunt died?"

To hide my turmoil, I said with my most officious tone, "I guess that's how some people tell you they're sorry because someone you love is no longer with you. Something to let you know that they're here for you." A transaction. The business of death.

"I have a half-dollar. It's in my backpack. Do you want it?"

"Yes. I do. Very much." I was touched. I didn't show it. I wished I had.

Jeremy smiled. "Okay, but let me finish this chapter first."

"Okay."

My elbows cemented in the beanbag, I could only look at my son sideways. I stayed with him, long after he had returned to his book. His small body sank into the yellow beanbag, swallowed by the slow, agitated sand. He slid lower, until, almost horizontal, he was reading the book as if he was looking through a telescope at the sky. Then he stopped sliding and let himself be cradled there. I pressed myself to hold this moment in my mind, like a snapshot, even though I knew this moment would become a memory, and memory would always change over the years, conflated or diminished, betrayed by one thing or another, or else buried until found. I just wanted to hold on to it a little longer. I felt alone in this. *Are you always alone in the memories that matter most?*

Then, Jeremy wiggled in the beanbag as he turned to me. "Dad, you're looking at me weird."

"I know. I just don't get to look at you a lot nowadays."

His eyes stayed with me, in an expression that I thought was melancholic. Despite the cramp I knew was coming in my leg—I was really too old for those beanbags—I wanted to stretch out toward him. My perfect aunt raised three imperfect children; I didn't feel like I had much of a chance with my own son. Yet that thought was making me reckless.

I pulled myself together and said, "Jeremy, there's something I've been wanting to tell you."

SOBER (WTF)

Colin wants a date, a real date. So I ask him what his favorite food is.

"Sushi," he says. White guys always like sushi. Not Japanese food. They always just answer sushi, like it's the only kind of Japanese food there is.

I say, "There is a place in Little Tokyo." I'm still on top of him, and he inside of me. His dick is warm but losing shape. I'm about to lift myself off. That's when he grabs both my shoulders. I push against his ribs. A reflex. Then I crumble. My elbows bend and jab him.

"Ouch," he exclaims. "Come here." A mock reprobation, all smiles and twinkles in his eyes.

"You caught me by surprise." I lower my forearms by his sides. His chest is a perfect landing for mine. We kiss. He sticks his tongue in my mouth, as he did during foreplay. I like this part. I wouldn't, if I had come. I'd want to be left alone then. But since I haven't yet, it's fine.

The place I take him isn't a sushi place, technically, but one page of their menu is filled with tiny pictures of specialty rolls. Shades of green, yellow, and red, arranged like mythological creatures on long plates. I bet that's what he likes. I bet he drowns them in soy sauce.

The restaurant isn't busy, not on a Monday night, not this early. We got a table right away, a booth close to the door. Through the storefront window, I see traffic beginning to pile up. When I look up from the menu after half a minute, the cars are still the same. The narrow First Street is just a long stretch of a parking lot. The pedestrians scurry across the screen, in both directions. It's like watching a disaster movie.

Colin is in the Army Reserve, and we only see each other after a drill weekend. Once a month, like clockwork. He always asks for the next day off, and the restaurant I wait tables at closes on Monday. It's a perfect arrangement, for both of us. I need a break from my NA meetings. He needs to fool around with someone else, just once in a while, so he can stay committed to his fiancé. "We have an understanding," he told me after the first time we fucked, but said no more. I never asked either, but I doubt the understanding permits a dinner date.

"I'll have a dragon roll," he says to the waitress. She often takes care of me when I come in on my day off, alone, with a book. Now she turns to me for my order, no flash of recognition in her eyes.

I order a katsudon.

"Do you want to split a sake?"

I shake my head. He asks again to make sure, and then orders a small one for himself.

Alone again, he says, "I haven't been in Little Tokyo for ages. It's changed so much." I nod to agree with him. He hasn't told me where he and his fiancé live. Just that they live together, which is why I have to host. He always says he's half an hour away. In my mind I imagine they do chores in a four-bedroom, two-story house in an LA suburb. Maybe he's mowing the lawn, and the fiancé is washing dishes, watching him through the kitchen window. Or I see them sitting on the couch scrolling through the tablet for showtimes in their local multiplex. Maybe dinner afterward at an Olive Garden. It's not my first time thinking about this. By now, I've assigned them fixtures. With each fuck, he gets new furniture in my head: an English roll arm leather sofa with one end that could convert into a recliner, a console table from Pottery Barn by the front door where he deposits his keys (except he never does, so he has to look for them when he wants to leave).

He asks, "Do you want to walk around after dinner? I mean, we paid ten bucks for parking already." He beams, half joking.

Dinner and a stroll around town—now I know this will be the last time I'll see him. A goodbye date to make the last eight months memorable. Around me are scattered senior citizens with their early bird specials and one family with two children in high chairs, one each next to an adult. The cool kids, the gentrifiers, they don't come to this joint. I consider my choice.

"I don't know. I've got stuff to work on tonight." That's a lie. "And it's a weeknight. I can't stay up late." That's the truth. The school district calls before 7 a.m. if a substitute assignment opens up, although they haven't called as often because I keep turning them down, on account of working late on those night shifts at the restaurant.

He splits his hashi into two and starts drumming carefreely on the empty soy sauce dish. "C'mon. You're not going to let me roam the streets alone, are you?"

But that's what I want to be. Alone. If I could, I'd rather take the train home in Cypress Park by myself than have him drive me. I'm sure I'm out of his way, wherever he lives.

"I need a tour guide."

I can't tell if Mr. Army Reserve is serious, but I no more belong here than he does. I can only tell him things and places that once were. One of the toddlers at the other table, the one on the father's side, starts to cry. Before I know it, he's screaming at the top of his lungs. The couple debate about something that should've been done to prevent this. The mother gets up and goes across the table, picking the toddler up and hushing him. "Okay," I tell Colin. *We'll wander for ten minutes*, I think to myself. Anything to shut him up.

He walks behind me; his hand hovers over my back when we try to merge into the stream of pedestrians. Even though he's barely touching me, I know to slow down when my body misses the heat from his hand. We walk like this for half a block, past the old, small ramen place that seems to gather a bigger crowd of adoring fans outside year after year. I've stopped going because of the wait. Cutting through those bodies gives him some courage. As soon as the sidewalk empties in the next stretch, he grasps my hand and hides it in his pants pocket, like a gem he's found on the sidewalk.

I let him.

To passersby, we just appear walking close, I think. The Japanese American National Museum is ahead of us, but it's already dark. Skaters are practicing their tricks in the open space in front of it. "There's nothing up there, really," I say. The signal has just turned and he pulls me in another direction, across the street. There are two men on the crosswalk sprinting in the opposite direction, probably our age, but better dressed: cool glasses, fitted blazers, skinny jeans. I've seen them get out of an Uber seconds before. Colin presses my hand to his side and says hi to them in a good-natured way.

We head into the Japanese Village Plaza. "Everything is new here," he says. Wide-eyed, he begins to rattle off the names of restaurants and stores on their marquees, or advertisements on windows. He tries to pronounce long Japanese words slowly, syllable by syllable, like he's slurring. "O-ko-no-mi-ya-ki. I-za-ka-ya." He reminds me of my old best friend, whom I stopped talking to last year after Step 9. On our first road trip together, my friend read all the street signs as he drove when there was a lull in our conversation. It was a long four hours to Yosemite to meet our group. We didn't know each other all that well then.

Outside a knickknack store, a group of young people speaking Mandarin are trying on conical hats and taking selfies. They scream at each other, all in high pitches, a little obnoxious in their drunken fun. Colin whispers in my ear, "Do Japanese wear rice hats?" I can feel his lips' moisture on my lobe.

"They aren't Japanese." What I mean to say is that they are interlopers, like us. But that doesn't answer his question either.

"Gourmet donuts. Cold brew." He goes back to reciting in front of a coffee shop. "They have cold brew," he exclaims. "You want something? Let's go in." Colin is like a boy in a toy store who's found his top choice on his wish list. He's too happy. Maybe this is not a goodbye date. Maybe he's left his fiancé. That'd be worse. I extricate my hand from his.

"You go in," I say. The line winds close to the door, anyway, and there isn't much room inside the coffee shop. He notices that, too, and doesn't find my remark too off-putting.

While in line, Colin makes a goofy face at me through the window. I force a smile, take my phone out of my pocket, and point somewhere to the left to make it look like I'm going to take a call. In response to my pantomime, he sticks out a thumb. I quickly step out of his view. I call my sponsor. The group of Mainland Chinese are encroaching in my direction, marching in three rows of three, cackling and shoving. I move to the open space that once was a pavilion, where they now are just setting up for karaoke, before Marie picks up.

But she doesn't. It keeps ringing. I look across to the dessert place on the other side of the plaza, its interior brighter than any of its neighbors'. There is no one waiting in line to try to get in. I had a lot of good times there, with my old friends, laughing, maybe even cackling a little. We used to go there after dinner, no matter where we ate in Little Tokyo, and hang out for a couple of hours, spacing out seventy-five-cent purchases of mochi ice cream, sampling different flavors. We got so loud one time the ninety-year-old Japanese grandmother behind the counter came out to hush us. Then, she smirked and went back to her other customers. Guess we did cackle.

The phone keeps ringing. I know Marie is out of the meeting by now, but likely giving someone counsel by the coffee urn. It goes to her voicemail.

I've gone to meetings for a good half year without a sponsor, before Marie forced herself on me. Now in her sixties, she's been sober for almost two decades. I had only known her to be the woman who gave out the chips at the end of a meeting, until one time she was called to give a testimony. She had arrived late to that meeting, having had a bad day at the DPSS office and then missing a bus. She was beaming at the front of the room because, as she said, these were the kind of things that would've given her an excuse to use back then. But not now. She said a few more things that essentially amounted to how she had surrendered herself to a higher power before she launched into her addiction history, the typical stuff about losing everything and everyone and hitting bottom. After the meeting, she came up to me. She said she had seen me all these months and I had hardly said a word.

I told her I didn't have the sad story everyone had. Yes, I lost my last job because of my drug use, and I had relapsed a couple of times. But I got a new job, even if I was a year from turning forty and surviving on tips. I kept my apartment, my family, and friends, for the most part. I didn't have a tragedy to contribute.

"Don't do that," she said. "Don't belittle your addiction."

I stayed quiet. It might look to her that I was being thoughtful, but no matter what I said, I knew she had a truism waiting for me.

"You don't look like you've completely bought into the program."

I nodded. "For one, I'm an atheist." I foolishly thought that would throw her off my scents.

"But you still keep coming," she said. "I have to think you're getting something out of it." Like a good salesman, she said I needed a sponsor in a way that made me believe I knew less about myself than anyone else.

She was right about one thing. I'm getting something out of those meetings. If it feels like I'm doing something about my addiction, I don't have to change anything else. But I was being made; time to step it up. So we meet up once a week for coffee, same spot, same time, not too far from here. I tell her things the previous week that made me want to use. By now I've been to enough meetings to know the usual triggers. I pretend to listen. She feels useful.

I steal a look at Colin inside the coffee shop. He's still third in line. Hands in his pockets, he cranes his neck to read the menu board, looking indecisive. Just then, my phone rings. It's Marie.

"Where are you? You missed the meeting."

"Hello to you, too, Marie."

"Where are you?"

"I'm not using. I'm on a date. And it's not going well."

Her tone changes, more softly now. "Do you want to meet somewhere to talk about it?"

"No, I'm still in the middle of it."

"If it's going badly, you should just walk away. Does it make you want to use?"

"No, no. At first I thought he was going to break up with me. Now I think he might want to go steady."

She doesn't say anything. I hear a car brake squealing on her end. She must still be in the parking lot. Finally, she says, "I thought we decided you weren't going to see him anymore."

I think to myself, *You decided.* But I say, "We talked about it."

"Many times."

"I thought it would end eventually, with him having a fiancé and all. I thought he was going to break it off. He was being all nice to me. But he's been more than nice, like we're really on a date."

"Listen to me." Now her voice sounds like she's in a tunnel. I envision her cupping her hand inches from her mouth, shepherding all her words into her phone. "You have to break it off. If he breaks it off when it's convenient for him, there's no telling what that's going to do to you. You have to take control of the situation."

What happened to surrendering to a higher power, I think. "But Marie, what if he's the thing that has kept me from relapsing?"

"That's just an excuse."

"I'm having sex." My volume is rising. "Regularly. Without using." I'm so loud even the Mainland Chinese are looking in my direction. For that, I add, even louder, "I'm getting great head. It's so good that I don't crave sex or meth for the rest of the month. What if all that goes away when he does?"

"You're trying to shock me." When I say I'm sorry, she has nothing else for me, except coming to more meetings. That's the point, isn't it? Unless I live the twelve steps twenty-four seven, the program is useless to me. Why can't she give me credit for my sobriety?

I tell her I'll think about it, seriously this time. "Can I call you later?" I need to wrap this up.

"End it!"

I hang up.

Now Colin wants ice cream. We've walked the length of the Village and stopped at the curb by the food trucks, on the corner of Second and Alameda. A crowd gathers around one selling Thai ice cream rolls. A camera is mounted above the guy in the food truck, chopping and scraping cold milk and mixed fruits on a frozen slab. Most are not buying. They're just watching the process unfold on the monitors at either end of the long window. Colin has his coffee but no fancy donuts, so he wants this.

"Ten bucks for ice cream. I don't think so. You're subsidizing the show."

"C'mon. Don't be a killjoy. My treat."

Ten minutes later, there is a new crowd, and Colin gets his order, grinning like an idiot. The rolled edges of the ice cream spiral like petals in bloom. "This looks too good to eat," he says and asks me to hold it. Then he takes his phone out of his pocket and positions it in different ways to get the perfect, artsy angle. His eyes almost cross to focus on the money shot. "Don't worry," he says, while he snaps a couple of times, not looking at me at all. "I'm not going to tag you on Insta."

As he's posting, I tell him I don't have Instagram. He looks at me suspiciously. It's the truth. I canceled all my social media ever since my own best friend said I was putting up too many depressing posts about coping with recovery just to bait likes and comments. We had a big quarrel about that.

He's picked up only one spoon, so I think maybe he took my lack of enthusiasm to heart. But then he scoops a spoonful and tries to feed me. He shoves it in my mouth before I can refuse it. We've done some questionable things in our time together, but this may be the most violating. Disgusted,

I wipe my mouth with my sleeve. I want to yell at him, but that's exactly what we don't need, a fight in public like we're a couple.

He takes a bite. The cold makes him pucker his lips. "Not bad, not bad." He takes another bite. With ice cream in his mouth, he says, almost slurring, "Man, if I knew Little Tokyo had all this stuff, we might seriously think about moving to the city." He winks at me. "I'll be closer to you."

"When are you getting married?" He said "we."

His smile disappears.

I've never asked him. I don't want him to think I fret about that. Everything I know about his relationship, he's volunteered.

"This summer." He's waiting for me to ask the next question: What's going to happen to us? What will be the new understanding between them once they're state sanctioned?

Instead, I quip, "Then I become the adulterer."

"Technically, I'm the adulterer. You're the mistress."

I laugh, but all I feel is a hollow cavity in my chest.

"Nothing has to change," he says. I should be relieved. He isn't dumping me. He isn't leaving his man for me. That's what I want, isn't it? Staying the course? But I'm mad at him. They can retreat into the comforts of matrimony and still live like cool bohemians. Everyone in the suburb or on his job will think he's a normal, stand-up guy. Everyone in NA will think I'm the home wrecker, and two days away from relapse. He says, "Man, I feel like I've fucked up." He must have seen the hesitation on my face.

I know I've been using Colin to stay sober, telling myself there will be a point when I won't need him. I can be on my own. It's a lie that I've held on to because part of me thinks it can be true. But I'm just buying time. Once he's gone, I'll tell myself, *Well, I've tried.* Should I go on with him for the sake of sobriety, even just for a few more months? Or do I take the break he's giving me, let him think that I'm too much of a square to be dallying with a married man, so I could get the party started again? It's sooner or later, right? Hell, I still have the number of a few people I used to use with. Isn't that the reason why I haven't deleted them?

The night is still early, and I haven't come yet.

I look south on Alameda. A block from us, at the edge of Skid Row, there is no business neon. Only headlights reveal that part of town. If I make it across the street and the next block, I can dash through side roads with urine-stained gutters where Colin would not go down to chase me. The flashing red walking figure on the pedestrian light is the only thing stopping me from running away now.

What the fuck.

I topple the container he's holding, spilling his premium ice cream all over his jacket. Quickly, I turn and lunge into the crosswalk. The walking man has stopped flashing, the traffic light turns yellow. It's a narrow street, anyhow. Only the Uber driver who was trying to beat the light and make a left onto Alameda is bothered, screeching to a halt. "What the fuck," I hear repeated out loud somewhere. I run the length of the next block and bolt across Third Street, wider but more deserted, without needing to dodge any car or person. Then, I make a sharp right and go down a dark street as soon as I can. Polyester tents dot the sidewalk. I slow my pace among the homeless, the parking meters chopping at the periphery of my vision. I can only hear my own panting.

The street smells of something once sweet that has gone sour, with an occasional whiff of weed. No sign of Colin, just as I expected. I stop and sit on the curb. I check my phone, and he hasn't even called. That's a surprise, until it isn't anymore. I doubt he'd show up at my door later.

It's over.

I count the minutes it would take Colin to clean himself up and take off. Or to avoid him, I can walk the long way to Union Station for the train ride home. I look at my surroundings. I brusquely put my phone away, lest I be tempted to call someone else. When I used to use, I partied with people who eventually would lose their house. They would disappear online for months and when they popped up again, they were living in smaller apartments in less desirable neighborhoods. I always knew, even then, that if I kept using, finding myself in an encampment like this wouldn't be that far-fetched.

And here I am, sober.

A man walks by me, shirtless. He wears a bottom scrub the color of the night sky. The muscles on his back throb when he walks, billowing like clouds about to give rain. He fiddles with the zipper on his tent and eyes me glassily. His tent, bright orange, refuses to fade with the night, and is easily the biggest on the block. Where did he get it? I can't believe it, all these new condos a block away, and I'm worried about how much a tent costs.

When I quit, the first time, my party friends were pissed at me because I had to turn them down. The few times I relapsed and went back to them, I had to grovel a little. But they always let me back in.

I take the phone out again and make a call. As soon as the other side picks up, I say, "I need to see you."

There is silence.

"Meet at our old spot? Please."

"Okay."

I retrace my steps back to Little Tokyo, this time taking my time and heeding all the instructions along the way. I pass by the ice cream truck, the scene of the crime. A whole new crowd, nobody recognizes me. The place is more chaotic. By this time of night, the people who live in the new condos begin spilling out of their freshly painted, modernist-edged buildings. I stroll through the Village. The public karaoke has started. A man is bravely belting out "Sweet Child O' Mine," in that empty space where the pavilion once stood, though decades of dirt still darken its boundaries, like chalk outlines. Turning his wails into more tolerable baritone, he even sings the background, "Where do we go? Where do we go now? Where do we go?" I stay awhile to hear him howl the last lines. A young man next to me asks me what he's singing. When I tell him, he nods in recognition. "My mom likes that song."

I say, "Fuck you," and walk off.

On the other side is the place that sells mochi ice cream. Before I walk in, I can already see him sitting, facing the door.

I thought I would get there before he did.

I sit across from him. He asks why I called him. I tell him I was thinking about our trip to Yosemite. I don't tell him what reminded me of it. Instead, I say, "Let me buy you something. Mochi?"

He nods. He has a small Styrofoam cup of coffee in front of him, the red stirring stick peeking out. Sugar, no cream. He tilts his head to study the menu but is undecided. "Green tea, plum wine, red bean, black sesame, mango," he begins to list them, as if the sound of these names would tip the scale for him. "Kona coffee, strawberry, chocolate, mint chip." He breaks away to grimace at me. "Who wants toothpaste in their ice cream?"

I reach across the table and cup my hand over his.

"Okay. Can I at least get two?" He thinks I want him to stop. Just the opposite.

I will tell him everything tonight. I will show him all my tricks, so that he can see through me. I will spare him nothing, as if words, once spoken, have that power to break a spell, at least for a night.

DUFFEL BAG

Cristina wants me to meet this writer friend of her new coworker, which is why we are taking the 1 to the West Village right after I get off a train at Penn Station. My duffel bag is not the easiest thing to maneuver in the New York subway Friday after hours. We can't find a seat inside the train, and I have to set it upright. It has the height of a small child, reaching well above my waist. Unbeknownst to Cristina, the bag contains all my life's belongings. Everything is packed tight like a sausage. I place my hands on the middle, where my laptop is nestled just below the zipper, lest it somehow slide to the bottom, where unthinking feet could kick and wreck it on their hurried way to somewhere else.

I could never say no to my sister. Not when there's a possibility that I may have to ask to stay with her for longer than a weekend.

She puts her head on my upper arm, like she used to do when we were in Pomona. We were quite a pair. Model foster youth. We spoke on the same conference panels. A picture of us smiling on a brochure somewhere. Our stories featured in her college paper. Her Latina face, my Asian one. To everyone else, we were the what's possible. To our old foster siblings, we were the exceptions that prove the rule.

In the clutter of the train, when it's about to slow down, she asks me about the book.

I say, "I just got the second round of copyedits. I need to work on it this weekend."

"I'm so excited for you," she says and puts her arms around me, squeezing harder than necessary. "Your first book."

I make a face at her like I had just tasted something sour. When she loosens her vise, I say, "The book might not lead to anything. There are so many books out there." I have a litany of spells I use to temper people's enthusiasm for my oncoming achievement: it's from a small publisher, short story collections don't sell, and really, coming-of-age stories are so overdone, and the ones about gay Asian foster kids do not exactly scream mass market appeal. Cristina has heard all of these, in rotation.

"Listen," she says. A handful of people have gotten off at this station, but more are streaming in, scraping my back without fail. I clutch my duffel bag as if that was where the anxiety was coming from. She pauses until I look straight at her. "Keep thinking this way and nothing will happen. You need to put out some positive energy. Don't be afraid to tell the universe what you want." There is that positive attitude that got her invited so many times to speak in front of at-risk youth: other foster kids, kids coming out of juvie, first-gen college students. It was no coincidence that she moved to New York last year to work on probation reform. "We're going to be the model for the rest of the country," she gushed to me even before she took the job offer. When she sighs, I realize I must have been wincing at her cheerleading for my good fortunes. "At least give me this weekend," she says.

She introduces me to her coworker Fidel at the Shake Shack in West Village. When we settle into the queue, the guy makes a joke that I've heard too often: Cristina and I look nothing alike. If we had asked a stranger to identify the siblings in our group of three, they would point to Cristina and Fidel: same race, same skin tone. Except for the way he looks at her—there is nothing brotherly about that. Fidel laughs immediately after he makes the joke, to let me know he is in on it, that he doesn't think we are related. He also says Devesh, his writer friend, is going to meet us at the theater after dinner.

"He was on a roll or something. I probably called and disrupted his creative flow," Fidel says. "He's working on his novel. His second. His first was nominated for a Lambda award a few years ago." He looks at me when he says this, like it was some industry speak that only other writers understand. Then, to Cristina, he asks, "You still wanna watch the movie, right?"

"Yeah, sure," Cristina answers casually, like he had just asked her if she wanted ketchup on her fries.

"What movie?"

Fidel says, "I don't know much about it either. It's a Lebanese film and was nominated for the Oscar. About some kid who sues his parents. Or something like that. It's supposed to be real good."

Then it is our turn to order our food. He and Cristina do this dance where he seems to want to pay for her, but then she declines because she's going to buy me dinner. While he's at the counter, I whisper at her ear, "Movie?"

"I think it's actually about child migrant workers in the Middle East. Supposedly very timely."

"A story about poor and possibly abused kids. Sign me up. I don't care about the movie. I thought we were just having drinks."

"After the movie, yeah? It's too early for drinks. It's New York."

"This is dinner, movie, *and* drinks then."

"You can't drink on an empty stomach. Don't worry. I know you're still a struggling writer. I'll pay for everything this weekend. I'm just so happy you're visiting me!"

Devesh never shows up. The usher at the theater wants to check my bag.

"Are you serious?" I ask. I have this vision of everything spilling out like guts once I unzip the bag, irretrievably unassembled.

"You're not packing a rifle in there, are you?" He says it jokingly. Half-jokingly. I'm beginning to get sick of New Yorkers' jokes. I want to tell him, *Yes, I'm a terrorist. And I'm going to strike terror at the heart of your precious country by hitting up a one-hundred-capacity theater showing a subtitled film.* I think better of it and lift the bag to the waist level. If he wants to inspect it, he'll have to open the bag himself. He just pads it down, gingerly, like he's afraid he would detonate a bomb. Then he lets me go, probably deducing that by the time I could remove a rifle from the tightly wound bag, his shift would be over.

There are twenty of us in that screening room. My duffel bag could have its own row.

After the movie, I agree to one drink. I've played the chaperone the whole evening. I might as well just stick it out a while longer and give this young couple a fighting chance. Fidel orders a whiskey neat, and Cristina a glass of pinot. I think it's not too on the nose to ask for a sidecar for myself. All on Fidel's tab. I park my duffel bag beneath the bar counter. I have to shift it a little to my side, so Cristina won't step on my laptop. Fidel is giving his recommendations on anything from museums to restaurants to Broadway plays. I feign interest. I have to be here just enough to keep them talking without either of them feeling awkward. This way, he could talk about his city without coming off as bragging, and Cristina could talk about her younger days, like it was just us reminiscing, and not her revealing too much too soon. Actually I prefer this to the double date they've arranged behind my back. Someone to keep me occupied, someone I would have to talk to.

Worse, another *writer* I would have to talk to. About our *craft*.

On the subway finally to Brooklyn, she puts her head against my upper arm again. This time we're sitting, my bag lying prone next to our feet.

She only had a glass of wine. She nursed that through Fidel's three drinks. With each he became more animated, and she more reserved. She puts her hand on mine and our fingers interlace. I can almost feel her head getting ready to nod.

"Don't fall asleep," I tell her. "I don't know where we're going."

"We still have a long ways to go." After a moment of quiet, she asks, "What do you think of Fidel?" Not that I'm acknowledging her question, but she quickly says, "Don't answer that." It's another few minutes before she says something again. "We have to be very quiet when we go into my room." I close my hand at this sentence, unwittingly squeezing her fingers. She lifts her head and explains, "I don't want to wake my roommate and her kid." Then she drops her head on me again.

"Tell me what our stop is. Then you can go to sleep."

"Forty-Fifth." She points to the panel where all the stations are lined up like a snake. "Sunset Park. Where the Asians and Latinos coexist."

"We'll fit right in," I joke.

"Yes, we will."

I roll off Cristina's futon just after seven. Her body is pressed against the wall her side of the bed is pushed to, almost like a magnet to a fridge, below the window. The bars of the fire escape give the illusion that we are trapped. I fall next to my duffel bag, still wrapped as tight as a punching bag. A space heater hums another couple of feet away. But without the blanket now, I can feel the New York cold in my extremities not covered by my long johns. I put one arm and one leg over the bag and pull it closer to me. When I start to enjoy it a little too much, it's time to get up.

I have come to New York because I had to move out of my apartment in Chicago, where I had stayed after getting my MFA four years ago. My roommate was getting married and his name was on the lease. The landlord was going to raise the rent by over a thousand dollars, and I couldn't find anyone to replace my roommate, so I had to move out, too. Even if all the ethnic enclaves in Chicago weren't already getting gentrified, I didn't have enough to put down a security deposit and a first month anywhere. I had less than a hundred dollars in the bank. The money I made—half-time as a receptionist at a yoga studio, tutoring gigs, carrying trays of hors d'oeuvre occasionally at galleries and rich people's homes and getting paid under the table—barely covered my monthly expenses. I had no one to ask for a loan. A few times, when we were undergrads, I asked Cristina for twenty or forty bucks before a payday. After I left for grad school, the distance between us also made this kind of favor harder to ask. I doubt she had much saved up anymore, what with her being unemployed in LA for a month before finding this job in New York and all the expenses moving here. When my publisher sent me $500, the first installment of my advance after turning in my revised manuscript, I decided to take the train here and suss out her living arrangement. I told her I'd visit for the weekend. I'm certain she will let me stay for a week. She would love it, in fact. Longer, if we turned out to be as laid back as adults as when we were young. And if her roommates were not psychos. This is a recon mission of sorts.

I put on yesterday's clothes, fish out the novel I've been reading from my bag, pick up Cristina's keys on her desk, and slip out of the room. The common area is just a long stretch of open space. The kitchen is right outside of Cristina's bedroom. Nothing remarkable—an old stove with dials that were rubbed blank from use, a round table with enough seating for four, and an open pantry shelving unit with an assortment of pots and pans anchoring on the bottom. It is joined by the living room. Except for the keyboard and the couch (another futon), the three walls are lined with columns of bookshelves, with as many books as there are magazine files and baskets of craft supplies, each affixed with a notecard label by a clothespin. The series of bookshelves are broken by three doors, one we walked through last night and the other two, presumably, leading to the mother and son, respectively. Nothing stirs behind any of them.

I walk down two flights of stairs and exit their brownstone. Ice cakes on the bottom of every tree that lines the sidewalks. The branches are bare and desperately reaching to the cloudy sky. I close my trench coat around me. I've been wearing this almost every day this winter. I worry about the smell that might emanate from it, which I might be too familiar to catch. I stop at a coffee house to buy a steaming cup of dark roast and read my book for fifteen minutes. Two blocks away, I find a corner store. I buy three potatoes, a red pepper, a jalapeño, a small brown onion, a package of bacon, and half a dozen eggs. All for less than fifteen dollars. Time to make a good first impression.

Back home, no one is up yet. The kitchen is almost as cold as the outside, so I turn on the oven, readying it for the bacon. I find half a bulb of garlic on the counter and a handful of wilting, prewashed spinach in a rolled-up plastic bag in the fridge. I don't know whether they belong to Cristina or her roommate. I grab them, anyway. It's a habit. Even back in college with roommates who liked to assign shelves in the cold box or label their Tupperware with painter's tape, I took what I wanted. But I always made enough for everyone, like daring them to complain about my trespass, to weigh the rigid middle-class rules their mommies and daddies taught them heavier than my culinary offerings. At most we had house meetings. I adjusted my behavior for a few weeks, kept to my shelves. Then I was back to my old ways. They ate my delicious dinners and decided, eventually, that a few sprigs of cilantro, a dollop of sour cream, or a couple slices of hardening deli meat was a small price to pay for domestic harmony. And they'd just chalk up my lack of boundaries to my foster home rearing. This was when they would imagine I had to scrounge a spare kitchen for forgotten morsels or fight for every scrap of food in an overcrowded household.

I let them think that. It made them scared of me a little bit.

Out of nowhere a cat jumps onto the counter and catwalks the edge toward the window. On the ledge there is a plastic box labeled "compost," with the same handwriting as those notecards clipped to the craft baskets in the other room. Cursive, like a roller pen skating on a piece of paper. I drop the potato peels and onionskins into that box. As quiet as I can be, I mince the garlic and heat up some olive oil on a large cast iron skillet on a low flame. I halve the onion. Flat on the cut side, I slice it in the middle, parallel to the cutting board and almost to the end, and then bear the knife down so the pieces fall like Lego pieces off a shaky castle. I scoop the garlic into the skillet. By the time I dice the red pepper the same size as the onion, the purloined garlic sizzles beautifully. It disappears in the avalanche of peppers and onions. I turn up the heat.

I love mornings because things would not have strayed from what I have intended them to be yet.

I'm dicing the potatoes when a strange voice calls my name.

"You must be James."

I turn around and find a young boy. Everybody calls me Jim or Jimmy. Only Cristina calls me James, as if her refusal to infantilize me was a shield against the bullying from the bigger boys and the insults from stupid adults. James doesn't bend over so easily, like Jim or Jimmy would.

I wait for the joke about how I don't look like Cristina's brother. When none comes, I affirm, "I am James." He must be the son, although he is nothing like Cristina described. He looks younger than thirteen, and he definitely doesn't look French, like his mom, Cristina's roommate. His eyes are dark but bright, his complexion browner than mine. I couldn't tell if his eyes are small, or if he has not completely woken up yet. The white tunic he is wearing makes him look like a scrawny Moroccan kid. His hands touch opposite elbows, his arms forming a narrow, double perch right above his plaid cotton pajama bottoms. "You are Luc," I finally say.

He points to the book I've left on their kitchen table. "Is this any good?"

"It's all right. It's kinda slow but has its moments." What I didn't tell Luc was that the writer and I were in the same MFA program at the same time. I read three-quarters of this book in its first draft. He writes about the urban Native American experience, and our classmates and professors ate it up, so much so that they had no praises left for my hard-knock foster tales. His drunk Indians were more convincing than my orphans being coerced to suck cocks. I wasn't going to tell Luc any of this. Just to be charitable, I add, "His language can be beautiful." What a pretentious thing to say to a teenager. Also, I'm reading it to see if this classmate has taken any of my critique to heart. I'm looking for silent validations. Not going to share that either.

"Too bad," Luc says. "I was looking forward to reading it."

He is one of those kids, I guess, who draws his leisure reading from the Pulitzer's shortlist. I feel bad, from bad-mouthing a fellow writer who by all objective measures is a superior writer to me or from discouraging a young person from experiencing his voice. So I say, "You should read it. When it's good, it's really good."

Luc considers the book cover a while longer. Maybe he's reading the glowing blurb from Margaret Atwood or Louise Erdrich. I forget whose is on the front and whose on the back.

To tear his attention away, I say, "I'm making breakfast."

"I can make coffee," he offers.

"Oh, good. I hate working other people's coffee machines."

He jaunts to my side of the kitchen. "You take it black, too?"

Catherine, or Cat, Luc's mom and Cristina's roommate, is not upset that I raided her fridge. She even appreciates her spinach in my home fries. That, and the runny yolk from the egg I placed on top of the potatoes, add vibrant colors, she says. With her French accent, she almost makes it sound like art. I have also found some cumin and coriander seeds and taught Luc how to grind them with the pestle and mortar, which he swore had never been taken out of the cabinet in all his life. When I reveal the secret ingredients, Cat responds, "Very Indian. Or Mexican. It's very flavorful, like, like, like . . ." she was searching for the right word. "Sophistiqué."

"Sophisticated," I say.

"Refined," she points at me with alert eyes, like she was rejecting my choice for a sham copy of her French word. "And this bacon," she waxes on, "so crunchy and full of flavor, but not greasy at all." I think to myself, someone will have to clean up that rack, the sooner, the better.

Cat wears a long, threadbare cloth around her shoulders like a shawl. It drapes over her tiny body when she wraps her bony fingers around her coffee mug. Once she gets a little animated with her speech, she spreads her arms and it becomes her gossamer wings. She sometimes speaks to her son in French, almost a soft mumble. Then she smiles sheepishly at Cristina and me. She tells me about her business. An artist and fluent in three European languages, Cat runs an immersion program that uses arts and performance to help elementary school students become bilingual.

She talks endlessly about how language shapes the way we see the world. I'm generally agreeable to this philosophy, though I could only catch about half of what she said.

Maybe that is why I missed the transition. "Luc here was really looking forward to your arrival," she says. "We know plenty of artists, but you're the first writer he meets."

Language, words, writer. Am I expected to dazzle her son's perception of reality? Luc interrupts his mom in French. She is embarrassing him. He is correcting her. I couldn't tell which. Probably a little of both. I couldn't be the first writer the boy met. The mother and son probably go to readings for fun.

She waves him off and continues, "Luc just read . . . what was that book you read last year . . . the memoir about that songwriter who had a relationship with the homosexual photographer."

Luc and I both say at the same time, "Patti Smith, *Just Kids*."

"Yes, that one. He read that last year and became fascinated with writers. I know plenty of artists, but they're all local. That's not it." She turns to her son and asks him something in French. But before he could answer, she lifts her hands, her shawl raised like a curtain. "Pedestrian." She says the word like I would speak French, overenunciating it. "You called them pedestrian."

"No," Luc protests. "Some of your friends are pedestrian. But I said 'ephemeral.'"

I tell Luc, "You haven't read my work."

Cristina says, "Yes, he has. I showed him one of your stories. The one you published in some journal a few years ago."

There's been only three. I'm afraid to guess which one she showed Luc.

"Being a writer is not all that glamorous. To wit, I'm slumming with my sister when I come to New York." I caught what I said after I had said it. It could've been taken as condescension, but no one in the room did.

"I can't believe you both slept in that small room," Cat interjects. "You're more than welcome to sleep out here. We'll turn on the heater."

I make note of her open offer for later. Now I look at Luc and tell him, "Most of us don't become famous like Patti Smith. Or the people she writes about." Some of us might have to start tricking like Mapplethorpe, though.

"It's not the money, or the fame." Luc chimes in, almost demure. "You'll have something concrete you can hold that has your name on it. Anyone can read it. Even after you die."

Legacy. He's talking about a legacy. Not the first time I've heard it. There is so much this kid, as sophisticated or refined as he might actually be, doesn't know. People who don't know what roof they will live under in a few days don't spend the day worrying about legacy.

"See, brother," Cristina says. "You need to think like this kid."

Breakfast takes over two hours, with each of us taking turns with the one bathroom for our showers. While his mother is gone, Cristina and I find out a little more about Luc's heritage. We don't ask directly. We both had experience with people not so artfully asking us what happened that led us to being foster kids. The older we got, the more awkward those curiosities were. They stuttered through their question and acted as if we could see through their skull and find them entertaining the thought that it was our fault that we were abandoned. So with Luc, we know to wait for the perfect opening. If not today, then another time. But Luc offers some clues on his own, when he talks about when he started to learn the keyboard. Five years ago, he says, right after he came back from visiting his father in Sri Lanka. He uses the visit to mark time.

"Did your father play?" I ask.

"Do you visit Sri Lanka often?" Cristina joins in quickly.

He answers no to both our questions and says no more. We know to stop for today.

Getting ready for my turn for the bathroom, I go to Cristina's room and get out some clean clothes from my sausage roll. I also remove my laptop and a sweater. It's going to be in the low sixties today. I can leave my trench coat outside for a little sun. With a few things out in the middle, the bag deflates a little but retains its shape at either end. Like a canoe. If I could convince Cristina to do her laundry this weekend, I could sneak a few pieces into her pile without making my own load.

Outside, I hear her invite Luc to our outing to Central Park this afternoon.

"It's brilliant," Cat says. I imagine her arm raised high when she says this, like inviting a choir to belt their hearts out. "I have to get ready for my puppeteer workshop this afternoon. We can make dinner when you all come back!"

In my second year in the MFA program, I workshopped a short story about a foster kid who learned about his sexuality when he was bullied into sucking an older boy's dick in the home, all because that older boy's girlfriend wouldn't. He had grown to like it, even though he let this older boy thrash him a little so he could feign his submission. I had to sit and hear everyone's feedback and couldn't respond until they were done. There was silence at first, until someone finally piped up. "There's too much dick." A flutter of nervous laughter opened the floodgate. Someone said she appreciated me "trying to push the envelope between art and pornography," but the piece fell on the wrong side. Another person, who was working on a feminist retelling of *Lolita*, from the point of view of the titular character, said he was worried that I was portraying the abused liking the abuse. He hid his dismay behind an analytical discussion about the "subaltern" being superseded for their capacity for self-representation. Finally, a classmate stood up for me and said the story was "brave." In each of their own awkward ways, they were trying to figure out whether the story was something that had really happened to me.

The guy, who would go on to write the bestseller I'm reading, said it was an "obligatory blowjob story." The professor asked him to elaborate. "It's like the writer wants us, the readers, to be shocked," he said, "but it's the writer who seems to be more titillated than anyone else." I hated that he talked about me in the third person, though everyone did; it was what we were supposed to say in our critiques. But more than anyone else, he made me feel like an impostor. That I couldn't be authentic like him. As if that wasn't enough, when the professor asked if anyone had other feedback for me, the guy went and added, "Whatever." His last word.

I wanted to tell him I didn't know whether I wanted to smack him or to suck his cock. When it was my turn to speak, though, I just thanked everyone for their input and said, "Mostly, I'm just glad to have finally put this down on paper. I've been waiting a long time to tell this story."

You tell them without telling them. You tell them enough, so they can make up the rest for you.

The story is one of three I've published. Cristina couldn't possibly share this one with Luc, could she? No, I remember now. I didn't show her this one, to avoid her asking me if any of her boyfriends had done something like that to me. I want to ask Luc which of my stories he read, but that seems like an obvious ploy to talk more about myself.

"Is it autobiographical?" Luc asks. "What you write."

Trying to hide my disappointment at his question, I respond, "No. I don't write memoirs."

Cristina is on the phone outside, presumably with Fidel. I can tell by her smile. Luc and I are eating our pizzas at the counter by the storefront. I can literally see her smile. It doesn't stop, whether her mouth is moving or not.

By the time she comes back in, the cheese on her pizza has hardened like random paint on an abstract expressionist painting. She asks if we want to catch a Broadway play tonight. Fidel is heading to the box office to see about rush tickets.

Even though I'm ready to say no, I ask, "Which one?"

"*Waitress.*"

"The musical," Luc adds unenthusiastically.

"The one based on the movie?" I ask.

She knows that tone. "It wasn't that bad of a movie. And you're in New York. What's wrong with seeing a Broadway musical?"

"I'm going to pass."

"Me, too," says Luc.

"I'm trying to save money, Cris."

"C'mon. Fidel will pay."

"That's weird."

"Fine. He's paying for me. I'll pay for you. And you, too, Luc."

I say, "No, thanks." I would tell Luc to make up his own mind, but I doubt he's the type of kid who likes to see anything where adults would burst into songs when they speak.

"Do you mind if I go with Fidel then?"

"Um . . . okay."

"I mean, you could take Luc home, right?"

"I'm a stranger here. Technically, Luc will be taking me home."

"Okay. Let me call Fidel before he buys too many tickets."

She leaves again, this time taking the pizza with her.

Luc catches me looking after her. He says, "Maybe there aren't any tickets left."

How is a thirteen-year-old more perceptive than my own sister? It is then I realize Cristina is falling in love, the worst kind of love, the kind at the early phase when you don't see anything else.

Luc and I settle in a coffee shop on the Upper West Side so I can get some work done. Cristina kisses him on his head before she leaves us. Turning to me, she just says she'll see me later. Luc orders a cortado. Half milk, half espresso, a strange choice for a kid who drinks his coffee black. It comforts me. It reminds me that I was young once, too, and makes me feel a little warmer toward my sister. After all, I did have a childhood, and it wasn't all stuff in a case file. Whatever fragments I can hold on to now, I can do that because of her. I'm still undecided, though, about asking to stay with her. And she'll probably say yes now, having abandoned me on the first day I'm here. Why do I resist asking her?

I take out my laptop from the cloth bag I've borrowed from Cristina and then the book, which I've been using to cushion the laptop. I give the book to Luc to read. The first chapter is good, like most first chapters are.

In our second round, my copyeditor has about two dozen questions for me, down from a list of three hundred. *Pick the box up. Pick up the box.* Okay. *Over thirty people came. More than thirty people came.* Okay. Just get it done. I don't want these babies anymore. Put them out on the market. Maybe even in time to apply for a residency in the fall. Somewhere not so cold would be nice, but I'm not picky.

Luc chuckles out loud. I think I know the passage he just read.

Rewrite for clarity? Fine. I copy and paste the paragraph in question onto a blank document. I scramble the words. Oil up the wilting ones. Grind the others to release their flavor. *Voilà. Sophistiqué.*

I press send, with the sinking feeling that no one is going to buy them. The world is not ready for boys who like blowjobs.

We're walking back toward the park on our way to the subway station. We stop at the intersection. When the light changes, just as I'm about to step into the street, two cyclists swoosh by, almost clipping me. A young man next to me has to take a step back onto the sidewalk, too. His baseball cap casts a shadow over his eyes. He turns to me and, flashing a conspiratorial grin, says, "You can take a guy out of the ghetto, but you can't . . ." The cyclists were Black. The young man pauses when he sees Luc by my side and probably my eyes seething. In my mind, I finish the joke for him. I even imagine him ending with, "Amirite?" the way any jerkface New Yorker would. Out loud, I say, "Suck my dick."

He's taken aback for a second. When he recovers, he says, "Whatever," and goes on his merry way across the street.

We walk behind him. I have to hear this on the Upper West Side? And that shitty grin. For a second, he thinks I'm part of his tribe? I'm steaming mad. Mad at what passes for humor in the city. Madder by the second, by the tuft of chestnut-colored hair that peeks through the hole above the adjusting band in his baseball cap, by the underside of his cheek blotched with acne. Halfway through the intersection, I want to grab his shoulder, turn him around, and set the record straight. But what else could I say? I'm a soon-to-be-published writer who has run out of words. Instead, I pick up two steps, close my right hand into a fist, and land it somewhere between his ear and his neck.

It's a shitty move. I should've punched him from the front so nobody could call me a coward. It does the trick, anyhow. He falls to the ground, but he grabs my foot. I kick wildly, trying to lose him. Another pedestrian grabs my arms. He's telling someone to help him restrain me. It probably looks as if I'm trying to kick the asshole. I hop on my only free limb hopelessly. "Go, go home," I scream at Luc. The traffic is stopped on my account. Cars are honking. I drop my bag in the struggle and hear the metal of my laptop colliding into the asphalt. Luc still has my book. I curse at my enemies and somehow manage to exhort Luc to flee the scene at the same time.

Then I hear the sound that, once heard, would reverberate in the chambers of any foster's hearts—the sirens.

At the arraignment hearing Monday morning, the details are hazy to me. This much I know: I was booked a couple of hours after the incident. I got to make my one call still later, but by then I could tell Cristina had already found out from Luc what happened. She and Fidel had just sat down in the theater. They came to the precinct right away, but that being a Saturday night, I had not been processed yet. And nothing could be done the next day, Sunday. Somehow, by Monday morning, arrangements were made on my behalf. Devesh—of course, he's a lawyer, too—laid it out for me. It's the best deal. Indeed, it isn't a bad one. He told me to leave the talking to him.

As I stand in front of the judge, she repeats the agreement in front of the lawyers on both sides. They have agreed to a battery misdemeanor charge. (I had not used a weapon, and the injury to the young man was minor. He has to go back to school next week—he attends Brown, no surprise—and he didn't want to waste any more time testifying as a witness against me. Luc heard what he said to me, and Devesh thought it would not look good on the young man. In this day and age, punching someone who said what he had said could be seen as a virtue in half of social media. He was willing to let it go if I pled guilty to the charge.)

Yes, your honor.

Yes, your honor.

The judge asks if I understand the charge.

Yes, your honor.

She continues. For the sentence, $2,000 in fines and forty hours of community service. (At the agency that Fidel and Cristina work at—they are already court-approved to handle these kinds of cases.)

Yes, your honor.

All these years, I had no records as a minor, as a ward of the state. Clean as a whistle. Fuck the guy who said it gets better.

Oh, that was me.

As I enter the front door, flanked by Cristina, I immediately see that Cat has made good on her offer. She's hung a string across the living room like a clothesline and dangled her thin shawl from it, held every six inches with a clothespin. She moves the shawl back and forth to show me the section she's cordoned off. Behind it she's flattened the futon and from somewhere she's gathered a harem of pillows.

They tell me to take a shower first and we can go to lunch. In Cristina's room, I find my duffel bag eviscerated. Clothes are strewn everywhere. I've wrapped two boxes with these clothes, and the boxes now sit neatly on her desk, one on top of the other.

She comes up behind me and says, "I'm sorry. We needed to find money to pay for your . . . I thought I could find some in your bag."

She knows now. And I know she knows. We both know what a runaway bag looks like.

She stands tiptoed to put her chin on my shoulder. By my ear she says, "You weren't going back to Chicago, were you?"

I shake my head and turn to her to relieve her strain. And mine.

"How did you find enough money? I know I didn't have it."

"Everybody chips in a little. Fidel says a dinner date is cheaper." She chuckles.

"And Cat, too?"

She nods. "She said you were looking out for Luc."

But was I? I think I hit the guy pretty much because he said "whatever." Maybe I was a bomb, and the guy just happened to be there when I exploded. I kneel to stuff some of the clothes back into the bag. But it is futile. My duffel bag is a hunted animal, gutted and picked at. My poor shape-shifting daemon, it's no more.

"You can't leave now." She squats next to me to fold some of the clothes. "Not until you pay us back. This is your village now."

I nod but don't say anything out loud. The cat jumps into my pile of clothes and nests there. She looks away from us like we weren't there, like this is where she belongs no matter what changes around her.

I didn't punch the guy for Luc. I punched him because I gave myself to all these stories that would not change anything. I thought that the world was going to see me finally for who I was, and it would open up for me. Now I don't think it would. And I can't blame the world for it because Cristina's made it. New city. New job. New roommates. New boyfriend. New life. We used to be a pair. I'm not the exception.

I'm not exceptional.

Cat's picked her favorite Vietnamese restaurant in the neighborhood. A young man takes our order. He repeats what we say as he writes in his pad. He's in his twenties, a few years younger than me probably. I look at young Vietnamese men like him all the time and wonder if they could've been my younger brothers. Maybe the parents who left me behind got their shit together and had another child. And they took care of this one really well, to make up for their mistake. I'm never jealous when I think this. I'd be real happy if it was true. I smile at our server. He probably thinks I'm an idiot.

"It's this president we have," Cat rails, after the server leaves us. "We have Voldemort for president. These racists are coming out of the workshops."

"It's *woodwork*, Mom."

At night, just as I think everyone has turned in, Cat and Luc come out of their rooms and beckon me to follow them.

"We're going to the sky," she says. Luc gives me a mischievous smile. By their smiles, you can tell they're related.

They knock on Cristina's room and ask if they can go through her window. A look of recognition flashes across Cristina's face. She gets out of their way and they lift her window together. Luc climbs through it first. Then Cat looks at me, and Cristina goads me from behind.

"We're going up, to the roof. The moon is full."

It is chilly outside. I hesitate but their smiles are intoxicating. So I take one big stride across the sill and find my two feet on the landing. There is plenty of light outside for me to see the ground, three stories below, through the grates of the landing. I scale the metal ladder to the roof, right after Cat. I make the mistake of turning my head. My entire body is well above the railing, and my heart stops for a second. If I let go, if my hands get a little sweaty and slippery, if I catch the right wind, if, if, if . . . But I take it one step at a time up the ladder, pressing my arch firmly down on each bar, until the top.

Luc is standing on a footstool in the middle of the roof. He lifts one leg, like a flamingo, as if to test his balance. The pose reminds me of a painting I once saw somewhere. The world has all gone up in flames. The one thing constant is the statue of Shakespeare.

We stand in a line below him, facing the full moon, still ascendant to its crest. If I look west, the Brooklyn Bridge is lighted up toward Manhattan, strung like Christmas lights. They dapple the sky at the highest height, where the clouds cannot completely obscure them.

Luc skips down and across the roof, and stops just inches before the edge. I follow him but stay half a foot behind. The women scatter in separate ways.

"I'm sorry," Luc says. "I felt like such a coward." He's looking down at his neighbors' mess of a backyard. "I didn't want to leave you there. But I did."

I tell him, "Don't you ever apologize for that. When you find yourself in that kind of situation, not of your own making, you run the other way. Don't do what I did. You have too many stories to tell. You have to tell them."

"You haven't read any of my stuff."

"Write me something this week then."

He looks up at me and grins. Right then, I think, the world may not open up for me. Maybe the world will demand more words, and I will not be so afraid of the places I'll need to draw them from.

Across the roof, Cat yells, "Do you see the bird?"

"What bird?" I ask, looking toward the sky.

Luc points in front of my feet. How have I missed that?

Cat comes up behind me. She says, "A friend of mine, an artist from Hong Kong, drew that in the late nineties. I had just moved in. He was visiting. He spent hours up here one afternoon. When he came down, he just said, 'I left you a gift.'"

On the ledge, there is a painting, faded, but I can deduce the vibrancy of its original colors: red, gold, and green. I can make out the lines of the bird's feathers, even if I can't tell what kind of bird it is. It's too majestic to be a macaw. It reminds me of a quetzal. Its head determined, its beak leads the way. The wings, on both sides, each span more than four feet, ready to take flight, in the direction of the bridge.

RAMPARTS

1.

The good times came to a halt when Robert, the assistant director, walked into the break room Monday morning. There were four of us with our cups loaded with coffee, too hot for the first sip. It was 9:15, obviously too early for a break, but we weren't afraid of being chided for consorting socially during work hours. It's just that people like Robert don't eat or hang out in the break room. If they are there, they want something.

And it's just like management to walk in on us and not even notice the laughter has abruptly stopped. "Hey guys, so I have an interesting dilemma," he said. No good morning. No how are you doing.

We waited for a second, and one of us tried to be congenial. "What is it, Robert?"

"So I have this rabbit straying into my yard this past week. It only shows up at night. I guess it likes this tree I have in my front yard. It has low-hanging branches, and the rabbit likes nibbling on the leaves. The branches protect it from coyotes and the neighborhood dogs, but you know, I'm kind of worried about it."

"You should adopt it as a pet."

Robert squashed our helpfulness right away (typical). "What do I need a rabbit for? I'm not eight." He pushed his arms forward and opened up his palms, as if to show he wasn't armed, harmless. Behind Door #1, a fifty-year-old divorced man with a fifty-hour work week, no kids, desperately teetering on the brink of being overweight. After toiling in nonprofit all his life, it was too late for him to try anything else. We thought his social circle was shrinking fast, like a flying radius of a hawk zeroing on its prey. We didn't mean to be mean. We were just afraid of turning into him if we stayed in nonprofit long enough.

"I don't know, Robert," Mr. Congenial said, determined to stay in front of our pack. By Robert's swift rejection of his suggestion of adopting the rabbit, the rest of us knew he wasn't looking for "input." There wasn't enough room in the break room to rein our friend in. He said, "A pet could make someone feel a little less alone." The rest of us sipped our coffee.

"I'm hardly home. It wouldn't be fair to any pet I have. Besides, the thing that I fear most is walking out of my house one morning and discovering its carcass on my doorstep."

We looked at each other. Even Mr. Congenial had no response to that.

"The rabbit did come into my house once, but I think it's happier out in the wild. Here, let me show you a picture." Robert fished out his iPhone and flipped through his photo album. He inched toward us and we helped him out by moving in, too, until we could see his screen without our bodies being unnecessarily close. The picture was a close-up. The rabbit was chomping on a small piece of carrot. Clearly his provision, despite his big stink against codependence. Its eye was an evil orange-red. Its snow-white body looked fluffy and round like a small throw pillow. Robert swiped to the next one, and then the next one, more variation of the same.

Another one of us said, "This is clearly not a wild rabbit. It's well fed."

This led another to suggest that maybe he could post signs around the neighborhood to alert its owner. Then Robert frowned at us, the way he would when we tell him a project was running late or a community partner was being difficult. We've learned the signal for the times when we walk into the room and things have already been decided. Democracy is a show. He was never going to do anything about the rabbit.

I heard bits and pieces of the rabbit story after that morning from different sources. It was a topic of conversation when we stepped into the elevator, or when we were on a ride out to one of our buildings. We danced around that line about the rabbit's carcass in the story's retelling. We waited for one another to bring it up, but what could you say about a man who supposedly cared about a stray rabbit's welfare only because he couldn't see beyond the trouble of washing its blood off his porch?

Publicly, he made reference to the rabbit only once more, at a staff meeting the following week. We were talking about how we had trouble getting the seniors in our buildings to participate in our activities. Some of us were advocating a different case management approach. Robert interrupted the discussion with a parable. He said he could've kept the rabbit, bait it with a trail of carrots, and maybe it would have a longer life. But clearly it preferred to roam free, at a higher risk of death. A few of us pretended he hadn't said anything and plowed on about nixing the upcoming cycle of health workshops about scary diseases. Most just gave up arguing. All of us were uncomfortable.

There were other stories we preoccupied ourselves with in the days following: one of us was going to meet her future Mormon in-laws in Utah; another's mother, in a long bout of dementia, one day decided to open all the canned foods in the house and throw away the tops; someone's kid's preschool teacher just contracted pneumonia; and so forth. Our debate, along gender lines, on whether it was acceptable to date your ex's friend after you had broken up lasted three lunches. Once, we noticed the prolonged absence of the rabbit story. One of us joked that maybe Robert had skinned and butchered it for dinner, which many felt was said in bad taste.

2.

I was assigned to go to a national conference in Chicago on affordable housing and community organizing with Robert. My selection was quite a controversy because a business trip was not budgeted for direct service staff, especially when it was an out-of-town conference requiring a few nights of hotel stay, and I wouldn't have to do much except show up. Nobody else on my level was asked to go, and I skipped over a few people who ranked higher than me, including my immediate supervisor. Some coworkers actually gave me the cold shoulder for days after it was announced. To soothe things, I told everyone about the inequalities I discovered while working with our administrative assistant to arrange my trip. My flight was not direct; I had to stop two hours in Phoenix. I wasn't going to stay at the posh hotel where the conference was held, but a good mile away at a Holiday Inn. I didn't get a per diem. The administrative assistant gave me a talk about ordering room service ("don't") like this was my first time at a hotel and I had never heard of gouging. To all this, my detractors shrugged and said I didn't have to travel with the boss or stay in the same place. To them, I sounded even more ungrateful.

I arrived in Chicago the night before the conference started. By the time I checked into my room and called Robert on his cell, he was already at a pizza joint with a group of other conference-goers. I could hear their noises and laughter in the background, though I imagined them to be a part of that generation of older activists, like Robert, who were now wearing suits and comparing vacation timeshares. He told me the name of the pizzeria. "Ask anyone local and they'd know how to get here. It has the best pizza in all of Chicago," he said, with that old worldliness. He said they should have a table soon, but if I was not ready, maybe I could join them later.

I unpacked and took a shower. In the shower, I thought about going online and finding a hookup. But by the time I got out of it, when the steam cleared, I wasn't feeling so sexy anymore, and I was more exhausted than I had thought. The Dodgers-Cardinals NLDS game just started on TV. So I cranked up the heater and watched the game with nothing but a towel wrapped around my waist. After the seventh-inning stretch, I got a text from Robert. They just finished dinner and were heading to a sports bar. I thought, why the hell not? If they were boring, I could at least finish the game there. Maybe Robert would even buy me a drink with his per diem.

Chicago was chilly in October. I was from Southern California and didn't know what cold was. Wind was not everywhere the same. This was like the sneaky, numbing cousin of the Santa Ana. As I made my way to the bar, it found its way from the bottom opening of my pants and up my legs. I had brought one pair of long johns, and I was regrettably saving them for another night. I tightened my body, and the other pedestrians, as if they could sense something, stayed out of my path, even though I had made myself smaller.

I saw Robert as soon as I walked into the bar. He was sitting on the edge of a high stool, one foot on the perch and the other on the ground. He noticed me only after I tapped his shoulder. He introduced me to his companion, a pretty brunette probably closer to my age than his (a toss-up, really). As if I were his son, he put his arm across my back and pulled my away shoulder toward him, tight like a lasso. I didn't know if he was buzzed or if he was using me as a prop. Either way, I tensed up like a rock. He asked me what I would like to drink. I said a Corona. He laughed, and the brunette did too, like I had just said their secret word. "I'm not even sure they have that here." He asked the bartender, who didn't have the same reaction that they did. He had it.

Robert returned to the conversation he was having with the brunette before I walked in. It was about the rabbit. He was getting to the third night, the one time when the rabbit felt comfortable enough that it actually followed Robert into the house. The rabbit hopped to his right, and then to his left, alternating like this until it reached his porch. He looked at the brunette the whole time as if I weren't there, with no recognition that I had heard this story before. Even the game on TV wasn't enough to distract me from the fact that I was taking up space there with as much purpose as the old VHS player in our conference room. He sensed my impatience and told me to head to the table about twenty feet away. There were already a group of people there from the conference, all supportive services people like me. He even instructed me on how to introduce myself. I walked over there like Daddy had just sent me away so the adults could talk.

To rebel against his instructions, I took a big gulp of my beer and introduced myself a little bit aggressively at the table. I stuck my hand out to each of them, right in front of their faces, until they took it. I shook hard, so hard that a couple of them had to stand up to modulate the wave of our linked arms. I said my name louder than I needed to. I asked them what they had been talking about, instead of waiting for a right moment to make my contribution. They were bitching about their clients. I told them that one time a foster kid who had just been emancipated wielded a knife at me in her kitchen, and when I tried to calm her down, she randomly slashed the air with the knife until it gashed my palm. I showed them the scar on my palm, camouflaged by the other lifelines. I stood up, so even the two people at the far end could get a better angle at it. I had to tend to my own wounds and call 911 myself, and the girl wouldn't shut up with her apologizing. Even then, I was glad that it had shaken her out of her manic state. For six months, I was not able to close my hand in a fist. They wanted to compare war stories? I was sure I was obnoxious. Good. I didn't plan on staying in this field for much longer, and I didn't care if the child reflected badly on his parent, the lifer.

I looked over to the bar. Robert was showing the brunette his rabbit pictures on his iPhone. I could see his finger swiping the screen. She moved in a little closer to get a better view. It worked like a charm.

3.

I went to the plenary the next morning. I was on time, even though I had to walk about a mile to get to the conference hotel. The ballroom could seat five hundred, and there were about fifty of us. Robert wasn't one of them. I picked a table in the back with two people talking to one another. One of them smiled at me, but neither introduced themselves. I pretended to be engrossed in the conference program. Robert wasn't there fifteen minutes later either, when the room was two-thirds full, enough people there for the organizer to introduce the keynote speaker, someone who used to run a local campaign for Obama. She gave what was essentially a pep speech about community organizing, so there was a lot of clapping and standing and sitting back down. Robert strolled in after the fifth standing ovation. The brunette followed him, a few steps behind, preoccupied with something shifting in her conference bag. A couple of people approached Robert before he could find a seat. I thought about time-clocking my attendance by walking over and saying good morning to him, but I didn't feel like it, since I wasn't the one walking into the middle of a keynote speech.

My office signed me up for a field trip in the late afternoon to visit one of the sponsoring organizations in the Southside. The bus driver took a detour to show us the side view of the Obama residence. We couldn't get onto the street without clearance, so he drove around and showed us the other side. He pointed out other nice houses that belonged to politicians and civil rights leaders. We caught up with the other bus several miles away. That neighborhood looked completely different. Even the autumn leaves looked decrepit on purpose, more dying than changing.

We went inside a building next to a church. I could tell they hired people who were former clients. The teenagers in their rec room looked at us marching by like an unpopular parade that locals had to endure.

We filed up the stairs and packed the landing. Like people who had hit a dead end, we didn't know which way to face. Robert made it through the crowd and tugged at my sleeve. He was with the early bus and saw us coming in.

"I didn't have a chance to check in with you this morning. How is the conference so far?"

If I were honest, I would've said, *Everybody loves their work. Everybody bitches about their work. Everybody thinks the world would move slower without them.* Instead, I said, "It looks like a lot of people are doing a lot of important work."

"And we are, too, in LA. You should talk up some of your success stories from home."

I looked past Robert and saw a child on the floor at the corner of a waiting area, playing with free Legos. He must have been about five. I couldn't tell if the only adult in the room, sitting three seats away, was his mother. They didn't look very much alike, but maybe because she was overweight and he looked fragile. He was building a wall from right to left with the blocks, about half his sitting height. Nothing fancy. He was running out of Legos. If he had enough, he could close himself in.

Robert followed my line of sight and asked me, "What is it?"

I was being half honest again. I said, "I'm thinking we should have more age-appropriate learning toys in our waiting room."

That evening I declined an offer to go to dinner with Robert and his friends. I figured they were all going to some place with tablecloths that would frown upon separate checks. So I wore my long johns and took the train to Boystown. From the station, I walked down Halstead, block after block until the rainbow flags started becoming sparse. Nothing screamed out at me. It was still early in the evening. I hit a Marshall's and loitered about half an hour there. I walked back the other direction on Halstead and picked a diner that was within my budget. I ordered a turkey burger and a coke, and ate while the restaurant started filling up with groups of men.

Next door was a huge club, the kind with two stories and about five different bars. Each station had a slush machine to make frozen fruity drinks. I asked for a Corona; the bartender asked for an ID. Perfunctorily, like he would've served me if I had shown him a library card. He then asked if I wouldn't like a frozen margarita instead. He pointed to the board behind him listing the specials with the tropical flavors. I said no. He said fine, just that a beer was more expensive at this hour. Immediately he went to the other side of the bar and fished a bottle out from underneath.

The place was like a mansion. I could spend an hour just walking in it. The rooms seemed well insulated from one another. I crossed a doorway and then, to my surprise, it opened up to a huge hall. There was a fifty-two-inch flat-screen TV showing footage from *Evita*. The room was filled with gay men singing along with Madonna and reenacting the balcony scene with collectively raised fruity-colored glasses. They were all white, as far as I could tell. Not just any white, but the kind that glowed in a dark room. After that selection came Liza in *Cabaret*. I couldn't name the song. There were men my own age who shouldn't know the words but they all did. I didn't want to stay there too long; my Corona was like my hourglass, and it was half empty. I made my way to the rooftop, with a small glass enclosure against the cold outside. As the bartender there, in his muscle shirt, was pouring something into a shot glass without looking at it, he leaned closer to the talking customer, also in a muscle shirt. He stopped just before the glass overfilled, without taking his eyes off the customer. Maybe his expert vision had noticed me on the periphery, but I couldn't tell from his indifference. I downed the rest of my Corona and put the empty bottle on the bar top. I went downstairs and found my way out, leaving the rest of the mansion unexplored.

On the next block I found a much smaller bar, a dive. A cute guy at the bar noticed me as soon as I walked in. Latino, Middle Eastern, Italian—it was hard to tell even after my eyes adjusted. He did a double take while talking with his friend, the second take lingering longer than the first. I walked over to his other side and ordered another Corona. His head turned in my direction, but not all the way. In a while, his friend craned his neck to look past him at me. I had sat there for ten minutes. When I finished my beer, I ordered another one and walked away.

But I stayed in his line of sight for the next hour or so. He found me no matter which spot I stood. I didn't want to work that hard for a hookup, but I wanted to give him a chance.

After another twenty minutes, as I began to evaluate my strategy, the man stood up and made his way to me. We did some small talk. His name was Danny. He told me where he lived, but I couldn't hear it over the chatter of the growing crowd. I asked if he lived alone. He said he was renting a room, but he had his own entrance. I told him I was from LA. He said he had always wanted to visit and he had friends who had moved there. Where, I asked. He mentioned beaches, Hollywood, and Disneyland. I would've rolled my eyes so hard if he weren't so cute. Once he ran out of tourist traps, I told him he needed to come so I could show him the real LA. He responded by slipping his hand under my three layers of clothes. You have nice abs, he said, without looking up at my eyes. He reached higher onto my chest until his forearm was buried under my clothes. You're wearing a lot of clothes, he said, chuckling. I kissed him so he wouldn't mock me anymore. We ended up making out for fifteen minutes. We didn't know where our hands were most of that time.

Danny drove me to his place. When we got close, he pointed out the different murals in his neighborhood and described the meanings of the mythology they depicted. His sense of place made me feel closer to him, like I could imagine giving him my own mural tours in different parts of LA—Pacoima, City Terrace, Leimert Park—and him loving them more than the LA in his head. When we arrived, we walked down a full driveway (three old cars) in the dark. I was in front of him; he was holding my hips to guide me safely in the narrow strip of concrete between cars and bricks. We were both a little drunk and laughed at nothing. He shushed me, and then laughed louder. He laughed when he couldn't find the right key to his back door. He mumbled something, but I couldn't catch what he said. It sounded like Spanish. He tiptoed once he walked inside. He was doing it in an exaggerated manner, perhaps signaling me to do the same. We passed the laundry room, and his room was to the immediate right. He didn't turn on any lights, but I could see the kitchen beyond. It was small, and the only table was covered with tins and takeout boxes and piles of napkins. It reminded me of work for a brief moment before he pulled me into his room.

His room was as cold as the outside, so he turned on his space heater. He started undressing me.

"How much clothes are you wearing?" he said, as he pulled my second layer off me and discovered an undershirt.

I kissed him until we were naked.

We got under the covers. I couldn't get hard because I was so cold. When Danny touched me, I could feel him grazing my pores. I pressed upon him for heat. We fooled around for a bit until I was ready. I fucked him for a while until I went soft again, because he kept telling me not to be loud even though his moaning was louder than anything in the room, louder even than the space heater. We slept for a little, me spooning him.

I didn't know how much time passed before he turned around in my hold and started touching me down there. This time it didn't take long to get me hard. But as soon as I penetrated him the second time, there came a knocking on his door.

It was a soft voice in Spanish, an old man's voice. I thought he asked Danny if he had anyone in the room. Danny answered no, and told the old man to go away in English. He was paralyzed until he heard the door to another room close. Then he sat up, a little freaked out, running his fingers through his hair over and over again. Clueless, I started playing with his back.

"So your landlord is your dad?"

"How much did you understand?" he asked and started putting on his clothes.

"I work in LA. Half my clients are Spanish-speaking."

"I think you should leave." When he was dressed, he threw my clothes at me. I was still slow on the uptake. When I didn't move, he became more direct. "You have to leave. Get dressed and don't be loud." He began to shove me off his bed.

I wanted to yell at him, but I just said, "Okay, okay, calm down. I'm moving." I held up one arm to keep him away, while the other pulled my jeans up, just to show him I was making progress. "See." I should've yelled at him, but the helper as always, I let him think he had control of the situation. I started walking even as I was putting on my sweater. I walked in front of him; I could feel his hand trembling on my back. I told him everything was going to be okay. He just shushed me. I thought he would give me a ride back, but as soon as I walked out his back door, he shut it behind me. I stood there, thinking perhaps he would come out in another second. Maybe he had gone back for his car keys. I knew all along I was lying to myself. I made it to the front of the house. I had so much rage. I wanted to make so much noise, but I couldn't.

I didn't know where I was.

My cell phone said it was 3:12 in the morning. The reception icon had one bar.

There was no one I could call. Except Robert.

I walked a few blocks with the faint hope that I would somehow, eventually, walk into the business district where my hotel was, postponing the inevitability of calling my boss at this hour. But this neighborhood was a world apart. The dusk was chilling. I could feel its dew seeping underneath my jeans. Then I realized I left my long johns at Danny's. I was naked and numb beneath the button fly. One precarious bar. It could go any minute. I had not seen a taxi for the twenty minutes I was walking. It was now or never.

Robert picked up, sleepy-voiced as I expected. He asked me what was going on, and I just said I did something stupid and now I was lost. I told him the intersections, Wolcott and West Twenty-First Place. "What part of the city are you in?" he asked. I said I didn't know. I should be crying, but I just steeled myself like I was making a fair request of my employer. I heard him whispering to someone. I said the neighborhood had murals, and that was all I knew about it. He muttered something away from the phone again. I heard a woman's voice say, Pilsen. He must be in Pilsen. Then he said, "Stay there. We'll come and get you."

Robert came with the brunette in her car. I saw him on the passenger side and started dashing across the road. But Robert put his hand up to tell me to stay put, while the brunette made an illegal U-turn at the intersection to get to me. I got in quickly.

"What the hell were you doing?" Robert asked.

"I went home with someone and it didn't go well."

"What the hell were you thinking? How can you be so stupid in a strange city?"

I didn't answer him. The brunette looked straight into the road ahead and said nothing. This was not the circumstance under which I would like to be fired, but if it had to happen this way, so be it.

"Are you high? You look like shit."

"I'm not high."

We were silent for a long while, until the car crossed the river and I recognized the buildings again. We were almost back at the hotel.

Robert said, "You owe Cindy forty-eight dollars for parking. There is no in-and-out at our hotel."

"It's okay, Robert," the brunette said.

They dropped me off. Robert offered to walk me up to my room. I didn't want to get a lecture, so I told him I was fine. As soon as I got into my room, I crashed into my freshly made bed, face down. I howled into the fluffy pillow and pounded the neighboring one with my fist, five, six, seven times, maybe more, until my cry gave out. I had a hard time pulling out the blanket tucked tightly underneath the mattress, so I overdid it and almost pulled my arm out of its socket. I scurried underneath the blanket finally and curled up like a hard tortoise shell.

I woke up with a fever. I knew this like my own name, before even touching my forehead. I managed to text Robert because it was already ten and I didn't want to get in more trouble with him. I went back to sleep.

At one o'clock, the registration desk called to see if I was okay—someone wanted to come up with some food; would I be able to get up and unlock the door? I asked if it was just one person or two. She said one. I asked her to send him up, and I could make it to the door.

Robert brought me a large white Styrofoam cup of chicken soup with one huge chunk of squash and carrot each. He sat there while I ate. The soup felt salty in my mouth, and the chicken made a rubbery noise when my teeth shredded it. Robert took out a bottle of Nyquil from a small paper bag.

"Just in case you can't sleep," he said, putting it on the nightstand.

"I'm not coughing. I just feel sore all over." It was like my heart had gotten dense overnight and it was hauling the rest of my body toward it like unrelenting gravity. If this kept going, my body would implode and I'd become a black hole. This was what it felt like, but I just said sore.

Robert nodded. He watched me slurp two small spoonfuls of soup. That must have taken five minutes. Then he added, "I'm sorry I accused you of being high last night."

"You have every right to be mad at me."

"I'm still mad at you, but I had no right to say what I said. How many clients you see are addicts? You didn't need to hear that from me."

"I'm sorry, boss."

"What happened to you? I don't mean last night. I mean the last couple of years. You used to talk about going back to school and getting your MSW. You don't talk about that anymore. You're still very good at what you do. Why do you think we sent you here this year? You have this calming effect on our tenants. I hear these things from your coworkers in the field, from your supervisor, but I also see you do it in our office. You make people feel listened to. At least you used to. There is a bigger place for you in our organization if you want it." He paused. "Well, not today. We'll talk about this another day."

I nodded in contrition. It looked like I wasn't getting fired, after all.

I was half done with the soup when Robert stood up. He swapped my key card from the table. At first I thought that was my punishment, house arrest. Then he said he would be back later with dinner. The weather would turn colder, and he said I didn't have to go to the rest of the conference. After Robert left, I took a long, hot shower. I dried myself with one towel and wrapped myself with another. I sat on the toilet in the steamy bathroom. I reached over to turn off the light. When the steam cleared, I came out and drank two swigs of Nyquil. I wasn't staying in a hotel with a minibar in the room; I wouldn't be allowed to touch anything in it even if I were, anyway. The cough syrup was the closest thing to alcohol in the room. I just wanted to go to sleep, to be knocked out.

I slept for another eight hours. When I came to, I heard a faint TV noise. Robert was sitting about eight feet from my bed and four inches from the TV, watching the Dodgers-Cardinals game. The Dodgers lost the last one. This was do-or-die.

I sat up. "How are we doing?"

He turned around and smiled. "Not good."

"How long have you been here?"

"Just an inning and a half. I watched the beginning at the restaurant and left my friends to bring you this. We scored first, but it doesn't look good now. They left Kershaw in for too long."

"You should've stayed at the restaurant when they were winning."

Robert smiled at me again. He seemed to be in a good mood. "Listen. Every sports fan is superstitious, but I've played that too many times, and I'm too old for this. I can't put every out on me. These motherfuckers get paid millions of dollars. It's not my fault they can't hit a ball." He dangled another paper bag in front of me. "Wanna eat? Minestrone."

"Soup again?"

"Don't be ungrateful."

"I'm not. I'm very grateful. I'm sorry you had to leave your dinner early."

"That's all right."

"I don't mean just dinner. I mean Cindy. Is that her name?"

He nodded. "Don't you worry about it. I'm meeting up with her and the rest of them later." He then proceeded to tell me about Cindy and him. They meet up every year in a different city wherever this conference is held. He's not looking for anything that would tangle him up, and the older he gets, the less he feels like sex is something he needs on a regular basis. This is perfect for him. Cindy? God knows what her story is. He doesn't ask. He doesn't want to ask. They're happy for a few days, and that seems enough to carry them over the rest of the year. "I'm surprised people don't talk in the office." He looked at me, fishing for information. "As you can see, I don't hide us at these conferences."

I shook my head. He seemed satisfied. I didn't want to keep talking about him and Cindy. So I asked, "What happened to your rabbit?"

Half of his body turned toward me. "It's not MY rabbit." Then he turned his attention back to the game. We watched the half inning in silence. The Dodgers got a couple of men on base, but that was about it. Robert turned down the volume with the remote when the commercials came on. "The hardest part . . ." he began and stopped. "You know when it rained last week? I chased the rabbit in the rain like an idiot and brought it into the house. He stayed with me the whole night. In the morning, as soon as I opened the door, he darted out. Imagine that. Between the pouring rain and a warm, safe shelter, he chose . . . It wasn't even a choice. What the hell? The hardest part was everyone telling me I should have a pet. Being a pet owner doesn't make you a better person. I wouldn't make a good pet owner, anyway."

The game wasn't back, but he turned the volume back up, anyway.

I said, "Not for nothing. I think you would make a pretty good pet owner."

"Hmm," he replied, not looking away from the TV at all.

4.

Back in the office, they asked me what I had done and seen in Chicago and were disappointed by my short report. My illness had become so widely known that coworkers would greet me with their condolences. Those who had made recommendations on places and restaurants to visit lamented that I wasn't able to experience any of them. ("Murals. I did see murals in the real Chicago before I got sick.") They were eager to tell me stories at the office that I had missed. When I pretended to have the sniffles, they would cut the conversations short.

A week after I came back, I was assigned to train a new staff person who, if I trusted the workplace rumors, would replace me when I got a promotion to work full-time in the corporate office. He was just out of college, tall, good-looking, affable, and eager to contribute; he was fresh meat. They asked me about him, and I found revealing a few basic facts would satisfy their curiosity. We had started rotating our monthly all-staff meetings among our buildings to get the corporate staff out in the field, and to, in Robert's words, "cross-pollinate." The rookie's first meeting was in our building in San Pedro, where he had grown up. When they found out he and I were carpooling, some of them asked me for a ride.

On the way, he asked us to make a detour so he could show us his old neighborhood. We passed by the row of strip malls that had been half demolished because the developers had run out of money when the housing bubble burst. Their insides were exposed. They reminded me of the Lego wall the child was building around him back in Chicago. As I drove by, I stole glances any chance I had and imagined the people who used to work in these buildings, when they were whole, as if I was expecting these people to climb up the rubble and sneak through the rusty steel frames so that they could take in this new view of their city. No one in the car said anything during this tour of the past. Neither did I. Though it was not the new guy's intention, this desolation comforted me; these ramparts were monuments reminding me that people do move on, that they don't stay in a sad place forever.

Just a block away from our meeting, I stopped at the stoplight. Someone in the backseat pointed to the car in the next lane. It was a family of three: the man driving, the woman in the front passenger seat, and their small child in the backseat, her cheek pressed against the window. She looked young enough for a car seat, but she wasn't in one. All three of them, even the kid, were eating some fast food still half wrapped in foil. The adults were sit-dancing to music that we couldn't hear, oblivious to the world outside of their car. Everyone in our car but me laughed. I stared at the kid, who held her breakfast burrito up to her mouth like a milk bottle. The driver turned and caught us. The laughter in our car turned into guffaws. He continued swaying to the music, almost defiantly. Our eyes met. I gripped the steering wheel at five and seven, tight. The leather stitching pressed the shallow scarred groove on my bad hand. I smiled at him. He might not know to distinguish my smile from the mockery of my coworkers. For once, I wasn't thinking about the missing car seat, the junk they were eating, or where they were going. The light changed and he sped out of our lives.

And I thought that was what growing up was, to see someone happy and let it be.

NATURAL LAW

There are no children in the playground this early and this cold in the morning. Stella sits on the lowest rung of the monkey bars. Each of her hands squeezes the elbow on the other side. Pressed against her stomach, her arms are a reinforced perch for her breasts. Herman lowers his arm and offers her a sip of his coffee. She briskly shakes her head. "I can't wait until summer," she says. He notices that she's uttered this sentence again, three times in as many days. Their world has changed since then. She lost her baby two nights ago. *They* lost it.

She shakes her head again and kicks up her feet, sending a sandstorm just above the ground. She was pregnant for only eight weeks.

He places his hand on her shoulder. "We'll try again."

She shakes her head a third time. He hopes she's not refuting his statement. It's obvious. They're young. It was their first try. They'll try again.

"Hardly anybody knew," Herman says. It's the most comforting thought out of the whole ordeal. He didn't tell his parents. Even between the two of them, they didn't talk about it much. No pros and cons about the baby's sex, no name, no talk of baby showers or safer or bigger cars. No philosophical musings about the shape of the world they were bringing the child into, or whether they would turn out to be exactly like their parents. They weren't going to buy books, consult friends, or sign up for catalogs. When they decided to try to conceive, they were determined not to be that type of parents. They merely took a look at their finances, and the numbers told them it was as good a time as ever.

The day before the miscarriage, Stella surprised him when she called her two best friends. In both conversations, she told them, "I can't wait until summer." Summer was when the baby would be due.

Stella's mother would say that she shouldn't have told anyone before the second trimester, that Stella was acting too proud and that is when horrible things happen. In the old days, old women cursed their pregnant daughters so they would escape the attention of jealous gods. Stella's mother considers herself practically superstitious: If the custom doesn't cost a thing, why not follow it? When Herman heard Stella tell her best friend in Tucson about her pregnancy, he winced. The only thing that kept him from saying anything before Stella did it again, with her other best friend in St. Louis, was the idea that he would come off sounding like her mother.

They stroll back to their apartment after Herman exhausts his coffee. Taking off only their shoes, they climb back onto their bed. He spoons her and reins her in, his fingers spread wide across her stomach. It growls.

"You're hungry," he says. He wishes he'd said it like a question, instead of sounding like he was telling her she was hollow inside.

She shakes her head. It's become an all-purpose pantomime: to desire nothing, to tell him she's okay, to stop a conversation before it gets too far. Her hair brushes his nose, strands of it landing on his lips. He buries his face in her hair. His nose finds that notch where her head is becoming her neck.

When he wakes up, she's gone. He's thinking about the article he was supposed to turn in to his editor last Friday. He's asked for the weekend. He's wondering if he can steal time to work on it in the afternoon. He hears Stella in the next room. She's on the phone, asking someone to come stay with them.

Later, when he's at the computer, she brings him lunch. It's a turkey sandwich sliced in half. The unevenness of the lettuce makes the top bread slope. There are finger-sized depressions on the bread where she's held it as she cut it. She puts the plate at the corner of his desk. Herman says, "It's nice to have you home in the middle of the day."

She takes the seat behind him. "Sometimes I wonder what it'd be like to work at home." He swivels his head but still has to crane his neck to see her. She's looking around the office, like she's never been in this room before. She continues, "My mother was a housewife."

Herman suspects this is the moment when she's going to tell him that her mother will stay with them, that in times like this her attention to detail and her charge-taking will be an asset. He keeps on typing. Two paragraphs later, he stops to review his notes. Then he realizes she still hasn't asked.

He tells himself that she's fragile and needs a little help. He says, "They're more common than you think."

"What?"

This time he turns his whole body to face her. "Housewives." And miscarriages, he supposes that's what she's thinking.

She shakes her head—*again*, he thinks—and looks out the window. "I don't want to stay home like my mother. It'd drive me nuts."

"Besides, you'll have to learn a whole repertoire of recipes."

"Doesn't matter, anyway. We can't afford it with just your freelancing."

"It's good that I'm already staying and working at home. You can't insult my manhood."

She laughs at both his attempts at lightheartedness, but it's all wrong. The laugh is too hearty for a wry remark. He thinks she's made up her mind to laugh before he said anything. He smiles and goes back to the computer screen. *Tell me*, he thinks to himself. *I can be convinced. There are many good reasons for it. She can take our minds off each other. If that's the least she could do, that would be enough. She can fuss over you until you can take no more. Then you'll return to me.*

Stella asks, "Am I bothering you?"

"No, not at all."

"Your deadline is today, right?"

"Yes, but I think, under the circumstances, Damien will understand."

"You'll tell him about the miscarriage?"

"You don't want me to?"

He should've said, *No, I'll figure something out*. He knows it as soon as he's said it. He can hear it the way she's hearing it. It's his cautiousness, his not knowing when to ask her a question and when to make a decision for her so she doesn't have to. She doesn't respond right away. She's quiet as she's getting up from her chair. Herman stops typing and turns around. Her face is blank.

"Only if you think that can score you a couple more days."

Hours later, Herman emerges from the room with an empty plate. He walks over to the sink and does a quick job of washing it. Making his way back to his office, he sees Stella sleeping on the couch, her body shrunken into a lump. It looks awkward, with her back so round that some of it sticks out from the couch's edge. He's not afraid to wake her. If in those few seconds he could think of something to tell her, he would go to her and straighten her out. If he had something to say, he'd climb next to her and shelter her and whisper it in her ear.

Herman sidles along.

As soon as he sits down in his office, he hears music coming from the other room. Stella has put on an old record: Springsteen's *Nebraska*. It comes on loud at first, but then she turns the volume down.

He makes dinner as usual. They have some leftover chili from Saturday, and he adds a few stray mushrooms from the fridge that would go bad soon. Then he unsheathes the last half of the baguette, relieved that it has not hardened too much. The chili bubbles like lava. He lowers the fire and slices the bread. Then he goes and kisses Stella on her cheek and tells her it's time to eat. She straightens up and runs her hands through her hair.

He puts two bowls of chili on the coffee table and in the next trip brings a plate of bread. She takes two pieces of the bread and lines them on the side of the bowl. They chew in silence. He can tell she's in a better mood. She lifts her legs to the couch and bends them so that her body turns toward him. He crosses his legs in a lotus position, letting the crumbs fall on his body when they miss the bowl. When he thinks he can, he puts down his bowl in the gap between his thighs and reaches for her. He plays with her toes. She lets him and keeps on chewing.

"You're done?" she asks, smiling.

"The article? I have a good draft."

"What was it about again?"

"Dr. Gene Ibañez. He teaches physics at Irvine. He won the Japan Prize this year. He almost won the Nobel Prize a few years ago. He still might yet. He's like the Heisenberg or Bohr of our generation. Some people think he's going to change the way we see and understand the world."

"Wow. And you had dinner with him last month."

"I spent the whole day with him and had dinner with his wife and son. His kid is eight. Very quiet, not like him and his wife." Ibañez was well into his fifties. He and Stella turned thirty-five this year. There is plenty of time to try again.

"What do you know about physics, anyway?" she says, but not in a mean way. Stella takes a bite of the bread. She beams at Herman with her mouth full.

Herman decides to take a chance. He asks, "You're feeling better?"

"I don't know. I woke up rested, I guess. My body feels different. I can't explain it. Yeah, maybe I'm feeling better." Then her eyes light up like she's just thought of something. Her head tilts his way like she wanted their heads to touch. "How would I know really? It's my first miscarriage." She laughs, satisfied with her joke. "I probably know as much about how my body should feel as you know about physics."

Encouraged, Herman pushes, "You know, the next one's going to be even more special. At least we know we can conceive, right?"

"Don't tell me that, Herman." She sighs. Her stomach deflates with that grave breath. She straightens her legs and puts the bowl on the floor.

Herman holds on to his but only plays with the food with his fork. With his gaze trained on the food, he says, "We're in this together, Stella."

She shakes her head. "Not right now. Maybe later, when I'm better. But not right now."

After several more minutes, she offers to wash the dishes. He replies with a wooden okay.

After dinner, Herman takes an almost empty laundry bag and leaves the apartment. The bag has only one thing in it: the bedsheet from Saturday night. The laundry room is directly across from their apartment. Before he unlocks the door, he hears a low rumbling inside. He knows the noise is from the dryer. He's glad to find that the washer's lid is standing upright, the machine unoccupied.

He can hear their television set from the laundry room. He can hear Stella guffawing with the laugh track. It brings a smile to his face. He drops the bedsheet into the washer. He can see the bloodstain, the size of his fist, staring back at him from the hole. In the morning after they returned from the hospital, he flipped the mattress over. He considered throwing the bedsheet away. He still might, after he washes it. He just can't do it when it's soiled with what was left of that night. He adjusts the control panel, deposits the coins, and turns on the water. It gushes out. The water seeps through and darkens the sheet. The sheet collapses. The water reaches the bloodstain, but the bloodstain remains a dark brown crust.

When Stella told her second friend, Anna, the one in St. Louis, Anna got so excited that she went out to her backyard in her underwear to find her boyfriend so she could share the news. Stella laughed and told Anna she was crazy. In that instant, Herman had the thought that Stella's mother would've had. He's a lapsed Catholic; the god he left behind can be as vengeful as the gods of his mother-in-law are covetous. That god caught up with him for that one second. He thought something bad would happen. When it did that very night, he was glad it had happened sooner rather than later. It was only a small part of him that was relieved, but he felt it immediately. He doesn't know whose fault it was: Stella for telling their secret prematurely or him for feeling relieved.

The machine started agitating. He murmurs to himself, "I'm a good . . ."

Dr. Ibañez is a Catholic, too, and not a lapsed one. He said there are too many things that physics will not explain. He and his cadre, future crops of prize winners, are merely approximating these uncertainties and codifying them into natural laws. Man may scoff at the jealous gods, but it leaves him with nothing to fend against the vicissitudes of life.

Next door, Stella laughs so hysterically at the television that she has to catch her breath. This time her laughs depress him. His wife is mending without him, and he continues to misjudge the rate of her recovery. At least Stella has her body as her guide. Herman has nothing.

The dryer bleats and gives him a start. He leaves the room quickly like a trespasser.

In half an hour, he goes back to the laundry room. When he opens the washer's lid, the bedsheet is wrung long and twisted like a rope, and he can't tell if the stain has been removed. He pulls it out, one hand over the other, until he swaddles the whole thing. With his foot, he kicks open the dryer's door. He sees a listless pile of fabrics inside. They are thick and colorful: bath towels, sweaters, tiny socks. There is the end of a string that belongs to either an apron or a bib. Back hunched, Herman registers these details and begins to feel upset by his neighbor's negligence.

Just then, a man walks in. He's short and stocky and sports a mustache. In one hand, he carries an empty basket with a broken plastic handle held together by duct tape. Herman recognizes him from one of the apartments upstairs. The man says he's sorry. Then, eyeing Herman with the bedsheet in his arms, the man smirks. It's the kind of knowing smile men carrying their wives' purses give one another outside dressing rooms in department stores. The man asks how Herman is doing as he lowers himself and harvests his laundry like a dog digging in the ground.

"I'm pretty good. The wife's home today. It's been a quiet day. It was cold. We stayed in most of the time."

The man stands up with a full basket.

Herman continues, "I was working on a deadline. I have a first draft. I think it's a good draft, but you can be your worst judge of these things."

The man nods. "It's all yours," he says and jerks his head toward the empty dryer, now a dark, vacant hole. He exits quickly.

Herman kneels and pushes the bedsheet into the dryer. He's attracted by the remnant of the last load's warmth, and he stays down. He starts to count the things he loves about his wife and promises himself he'll get up when he's done. At the top of the list, there are three things. The Big Three are changeless; they're the reasons why he proposed. Then the list devolves into a mawkish inventory of traits that only he would notice: the birthmark just above her left nipple, the curling of toes when she's frightened, the way she slaps his hand when he absentmindedly plucks his already thinning hair, the constellations she fabricates out of the anarchy of stars in a clear night sky, the breath she holds when he tells her he's about to come. One follows another like rosary beads.

It's the small stuff that fills him up. Loneliness is not a lack. He realizes it now like his own natural law. In this moment, it is love bottled up, too much of it, with nowhere to go. He puts his head into the dryer. The hole swallows him past his shoulders. Pressed against the dampness of the sheet, he breathes in that fresh detergent smell. He recites the list again. And again. And one more time. Then he backs out, stands up, and slides the coins into the slot. As the sheet tumbles, he decides he can keep it for a while longer.

THE LADY IN THE MOON

"You both owe me fifty dollars," Mom says out of the blue in David's minivan. She sits in the middle row with Grandma. I'm sitting behind her with Dad, who's been sleeping. I thought Mom was sleeping, too; her head was so still. I know by "both" she meant my brother David and me. But it's David who takes the bait.

"What?"

"I don't care if you don't give anything for your other aunts' and uncles' birthdays. But Second Uncle is a must. He's a bachelor. He has no children taking care of him. I gave your Second Uncle fifty dollars from each of you for his birthday. Like I do every year. Except this year I'm asking it back, especially you, David."

I can see my sister-in-law Ashley's head turn to David in the front passenger seat, and he to her. Mom continues, oblivious.

"So don't pretend you don't remember this year."

"You just can't give him gifts from us and then ask us to reimburse you," David says, a little bravely, I think. "It's for you as much as for him. You want to have face." He needlessly adjusts his rearview mirror to make sure I'm paying attention. "Mason, have you been paying?"

"Leave your brother out of this," Mom says. "At least he's been taking me and your grandmother to lunch every so often."

I don't say anything because I feel a cold coming on. It always starts from the roof of my mouth. In another hour, it'll spread down to my throat. David glances at me in the mirror. Ashley turns away.

Right, I'm the traitor. If he really wants to do the calculations, I'm always left with the short end of the stick. Every unwilling gift I'm responsible for on my own. He gets to split it with his wife. It's like that with Christmas: I give two gifts for one back. And in another five months, after Ashley kicks the bun out of her oven, I'll be getting one gift from David, Ashley, and

Junior, signed to Dear Uncle Mason, as if the baby had the sense to pick out the perfect tie or scarf that goes with my wardrobe. That's three gifts for one, and he wants to give me dirty looks in his tiny rearview mirror?

Ashley skips to the next song on her Spotify and turns up the volume.

Grandma asks, in Mandarin, "We don't know anyone in Las Vegas. Where are we staying?"

"Oh, my gosh," Mom exclaims in English. "She's forgotten again. I must've told her a thousand times." In Mandarin, she explains, though a little too loudly on account of the music: "We're not going to Las Vegas. We're going to San Jose. Your granddaughter is getting married. You're going to see your daughter and her family in San Jose. Like I've been telling you for a month now. Your daughter is putting us up in a hotel." To the rest of us, she continues in English, "Your grandma is always dreaming of going to Las Vegas again."

"Who's sitting in front of me?"

"That's your granddaughter-in-law." Ashley's family is from Hong Kong and she doesn't understand Mandarin, so Mom avoids using David's or Ashley's names so that Ashley won't know she's talking about her. "You were at their wedding two years ago. Remember?"

"When do we arrive at San Jose?" It's not the first time she asks this question either. Not the first time even this hour.

David chimes in, "Grandma, it takes about five hours to drive from LA to San Jose. Remember the last time we went to San Francisco to visit your cousin? San Jose is just a little closer. We're almost halfway there. We'll stop for lunch in a little bit, and then we'll have two more hours to go. You're going to have a lot of fun at the wedding. All that good food."

"So why are we going to San Jose now? Didn't you get married already? Your wife is sitting next to you." I knew he should've kept his answer short and to the point. Idiot. Now he gets her even more confused. He's going to be the kind of parent who tries to reason with a three-year-old, too. I just know it.

David and Mom yell at her together: "It's your granddaughter!"

"Right. I'm very forgetful these days." She laughs apologetically. She does this because they won't yell at her when she's laughing.

"Hey, Grandma," I lean forward and touch her shoulder. "Remember when you used to tell David and me bedtime stories when we were little?

There was one about the lady in the moon. How did the lady get there?" This is the story that usually brings her back.

"How would I remember? I don't remember anything these days." She used to be just forgetful with recent things, but in the last months, her long-term memories have been scattershot, too.

"It doesn't matter. We'll ask Dad when he wakes up."

Defeated, I sit back.

Another five minutes later, David says, "You can count this trip as your payment."

We stop at the McDonald's at Coalinga. Grandma loves its hamburgers and Mom its fries. We all just want to be quick and get to San Jose as soon as possible. David pulls into the handicapped spot, hangs the permit (courtesy of Grandma), and opens the door the moment he stops the engine. He goes over to the other side and helps Ashley off. The van is too high for Grandma, but we've brought a footstool. I'm midway into helping Grandma off when he throws me his keys. Mom and Dad are already at the entrance.

"Hey, lock up the minivan for me, would you? What do you want for lunch?"

"Just a hamburger is fine."

"That's all?" He turns around already, back to his wife, and I don't feel the need to answer him anymore.

When I'm finally inside the restaurant, I see David in line alone, making good his promise to pay off his debt. Mom and Ashley are waiting in line for the restroom. Dad beckons us to a big, empty table he's bogarting. It's a find because the place is packed with travelers like us. Dad points at the blue wheelchair sign engraved on the table, all smiles. "Look, it's for Grandma." He will say that when Mom comes back, and yet again when David returns with our lunch.

He's ordered Grandma a fish sandwich, instead of her favorite. I raise the issue with him.

"She shouldn't be eating so much beef at her age. Fish is better for her," he says matter-of-factly.

"Not if it's fried." I know this is all Ashley's influence. She thinks our family has bad old-country habits: MSG, salt, the wrong oil, can't go a meal without some variation of meat. She's having one of those premium salads.

I don't know which is better, fried fish or beef. It's processed fast food, for Christ's sake. But I just want to be spiteful.

He shrugs and ignores my remark. He hands me the hamburger I asked for. I could've switched my lunch with hers, but there are two more hours left in the van, and I just don't want to fight with any of them. Besides, the back of my throat now begins to itch. The sinus congestion will start soon.

At the end of lunch, David preempts me and buys Grandma a soft serve, her other favorite. I take care of Grandma when Mom and Dad go to Vegas, and we always go out for lunch or dinner. No matter where we go, we stop by McDonald's for soft-serve ice cream. It's our tradition.

"Let's go now," Mom says.

"We can wait after she's done," Ashley says. Right, we don't want Grandma dropping the cone and dirtying their new minivan.

"How much are you giving Carol for her wedding?" David asks me.

"A hundred bucks." That's a hundred bucks from one of me, to another couple.

"What?" Mom exclaims. "You're giving them the set of utensils I won from the office raffle! I told you." Two months ago, she showed me the prize: seventy-two-piece set of knives, forks, and spoons of a-little-too-shiny faux silver, probably $29.99 from Walmart. "And you don't even have to pay me back because I got it for free."

"How come you didn't offer that as a gift for me?" David says.

I answer before she does. "It doesn't matter. I've left it back home." There is no way I will put my name on that piece of junk. "Besides, they want money because they're saving up for a down payment for a house."

"A hundred dollars? You could have my gift for free!"

"Well, we're giving them two hundred dollars."

Sounds fair, I think to myself. *That's a hundred for each of you—that is, if you haven't included the name of your unborn child on the card.*

We arrive at the hotel and meet my aunt, who checks us into our room: one for David and Ashley, another for the rest of us. Mom tells her that David and I insist on taking her out to dinner. I stay in the lobby with Grandma while they're checking in. It has a fireplace and complimentary cookies. I give her a cookie but she doesn't want it. Instead, she tells me to take half a stack of the napkins and store them in my pocket for her. She can never have enough napkins. It's her one constant.

"Is the fire real?"

"Yes."

She puts her hands closer to the fire and then nods.

"Who are we waiting for?"

"They're getting the keys to our hotel rooms."

"Where are we?"

"Who did you just see now?"

"All that sitting in the car makes me confused."

"I know, Grandma. Right after we got here, someone opened the car door and helped you off. Do you remember who it was?"

She stares at me for a few seconds. "My daughter."

I ask her back, "So where are we?"

Just then, Mom comes over. "Oh, my gosh. Is she asking again? We're in San Jose. Your granddaughter Carol is getting married."

She nods sheepishly.

At dinner, Auntie talks about the extra work she had to do for the wedding planning, all because her in-laws do not live in town. She speaks in English, to include Ashley. She looks at her especially when she halts to find the right word. Left to herself, Grandma eats what has been given to her on her plate. I drink a lot of hot tea. It's the only thing that keeps me from coughing.

"Mom is eating a lot," Auntie says, finally noticing that her mother has not stopped eating.

"She eats more than I do most days," Mom says. "She can eat, she can sleep. Except for her memories and her walking, she's healthy. She hardly gets sick either. She's going to give me work for a long time to come."

"She's happy." Then in Mandarin, she asks Grandma, "Do you remember the last time there was a wedding in the family?"

Grandma puts down her food. "Of course. I'm not that forgetful. It was David's, two years ago."

The group smiles and laughs as if she was a newborn uttering her first word.

Encouraged, Grandma continues, "They're going to have a child together." I feel like coughing, but my natural instinct is to suppress it in front of Grandma. She'll hone in on it like a targeted missile and keep nagging about it all weekend. She won't forget a cough. I think I can hide the cough until the sinuses get worse.

"See," Dad says. "Her mind is clearer than you think."

"Sometimes," Mom retorts. Then, to Grandma, she asks, "Where's David's wife?"

"Stop bothering me with these questions. I'm not a child."

"All right. All right. Don't get testy," Auntie says. "We're here to celebrate."

"You always ask me silly questions. Of course, I remember David's wedding. He's my favorite grandson."

Dad interrupts her. "Mom, you shouldn't play favorites."

"She can't help it," Auntie says. "She's traditional. A son is always better than a daughter. I know. I've been her daughter for sixty-three years now. And the oldest son of the oldest son is better than anyone else, especially if he's going to give her her first great-grandson."

It's bad timing, but I can't help it. I have to cough, so I decide to make a run for the outside, even if it looks like I take offense to what Grandma said.

Alone outside, I cup my hands over my mouth and let the cough out like wild horses. I have more in me even when I think I'm done. The open air, even though it's cold, helps. I breathe it in and it flushes out the stale, old air in my lungs. I find the empty bench outside the restaurant and I sit, shivering a little.

"You're cold," says a voice behind me. It's Ashley. "You want me to bring you something from the minivan?"

"Won't help. The cold is coming from the inside."

She sits next to me. "Sometimes, Mason, I just don't understand what you're talking about." Her arms push against the bench, so her torso stretches out from it, straight at an angle. From where I sit, I can hardly tell she's carrying a child.

She says, "You shouldn't pay attention to your grandmother."

"What am I? Four?" She's being kind. I regret it immediately. She doesn't say anything for a while. So I say, "It's easier to ignore them if you don't speak their language." I smile, because even when I try to be nice, it sounds a little mean.

"Oh, trust me on this one," she laughs. "It's harder when you don't." She looks at her belly. "I'm going to raise this one bilingual, so she can be my little spy."

We've just had a moment. I want to cough again.

"Hey, Mason, are you really going to stay in the same room with your parents and grandmother?"

I look at her. The moment is over. I clear my throat.

"Yeah, I guess."

"Where are you going to sleep?"

"I'm thinking with my grandmother first. And if I have a nightmare, I'll slip into my parents' bed."

"Fine. I'm just asking."

"What's it to you?" I want to tell her that, once in a hospital, I had to help a nurse move my grandmother. Her paper gown slipped a little and I saw her upper body, sagging breasts and all. All I could think of was *I cannot let her fall, I cannot let her fall.* Sleeping in the same bed with her doesn't faze me. How's that for understanding what I'm talking about?

"You and your brother are the same. You do whatever your mother says, even when you don't want to. Except now that he's married, your brother has grown a backbone. It's called me. He uses me as an excuse. But it's not my idea to not see your parents more often. It's not my idea to move farther away. All of a sudden, I'm the bad guy."

She's crying now. I sigh.

"You know, we don't have to go back in," I say.

"Who are you kidding?"

I give her a paper napkin from the restaurant that I've been saving for Grandma.

"Where the hell did you get this?"

"Don't ask."

She shakes her head. I hold the napkin in my hand in case one of us needs it later. I suck in some fresh air. I think I'm good for another twenty minutes.

After we drop them off at the hotel, I ask David, "Can I borrow your minivan?"

"What are you going to do?"

"I'm just going around the corner to the supermarket."

"What are you getting?"

"Come on, David. I'm not going to crash your precious new van." I don't want to tell him I'm getting sick. The cold has stalled in my throat. I can stop its trek with some help from the pharmacy.

From his driver's seat, he watches Mom and Dad take Grandma inside the door. Ashley follows comfortably behind. The glass doors slide closed.

"I'm not that tired. I can take you. Do you want to sit up front?"

I lean back, stay in the last row, and do not say anything. He drives on.

He finds the supermarket that I told him about.

"I'll wait for you here," he says. I open my door and get out.

In the market, I quickly find my zinc lozenges, the ones with vitamins and echinacea. I pick up some cough syrup that will make me fall asleep and some vitamin gummies, too. I dash back to the main thoroughfare of the market and find that all the registers are occupied. I decide to buy some facial tissues, in case the sinus congestion comes later. An old couple is blocking my way. I say excuse me, but they don't move fast enough. So I graze the old woman and squeeze through between her and the weekly special display. I don't look back to see their reaction.

When I emerge from my aisle with what I need, the shortest line is the old couple's. I stand behind them and drop my merchandise on the conveyor belt. The items move mechanically away from me. Suddenly I feel exposed, my vulnerabilities apparent to the rest of the world. The old man slides his credit card on the machine. And again. And the third time. The checkout clerk, in her unnecessary apron, taps her fingers while he slides the fourth time. I give her a look. Finally, she turns the machine around and flips the card the other way. It takes. The old man looks at me and acts as if it has been the machine's fault. The couple move out more slowly than I anticipate, so I almost bump into the woman again.

When I'm done and walk out of the market with my loose plastic bag, I can hear David starting up his minivan already. I get into the front seat this time.

"What did you get?" he asks.

I hold the bag tighter. "Just a few things."

He takes the hint and does not say anything the rest of the way.

When we can see the hotel, I can't hold it in anymore. I need to say something to him but I don't know what, and I can't let it go. So I say, "You owe me fifty bucks." Which, strangely, is exactly the way I'm feeling about him.

"What are you talking about, Mason?"

"And I'm not counting this trip either."

He laughs. "Isn't that something? She's getting more ridiculous." He thinks that I'm mocking Mom, that I'm thawing the ice shelf between us.

"You don't get to judge her. You're not the one who has to take care of a senile woman every day. You know Dad is no help."

"And what can I do?" he asks. "I can't change that."

You can see them more often is what I want to say. But all of a sudden, I don't want to drag him into where I am. He is right. He parks his van far away from the entrance, away from all the other cars. For a second, I want to lay down my sword. I just want to ask him if he's afraid that we'll become them and what will happen to us then. And would it be bad that you're only nice to the people you love because you're afraid no one is going to be nice to you when you're as old as they are? But before I can say all that, he shuts off the engine and turns to me. He says, "Neither can you, you know."

Before I get to my room, I can already hear my mother's voice in the hallway. She's not yelling. Her voice has just gotten louder over the years. I unlock the door. And as soon as she can see me, she directs the conversation at me, as if I'd been in the room all this time.

"It's good that you've come back," she says. Dad is reading the Bible from the hotel dresser. "Your grandmother almost fell. I told her not to move when I'm in the bathroom. I was gone for five minutes. She got up from the sofa. She said she had to pick up the jacket that fell on the ground. When I walked out, she was trying to sit back on the sofa. She backed into it, and she missed by a couple inches and almost dropped to the ground. Thank God I came out of the bathroom just in time. Of course, your dad was napping already. I can't leave the two of you alone for five minutes." She changes the direction of her conversation and is no longer talking to me.

Grandma is sitting on the sofa, safe and firmly in place, though she looks as if she doesn't know where she is. I sit next to her and unwrap a zinc lozenge for her.

"What is it?" She asks.

"It's candy."

She takes it from me. I take another one out and unwrap it for myself. We put them in our mouths together. I give her a pack of facial tissues. She grabs it eagerly. Even with the package she can tell the tissues are much softer than the napkins she takes everywhere.

"It's free?" she asks.

I nod.

Then I take everything else and grab my pajamas and go into the bathroom. I turn on the shower and take a swig of the cough syrup and hide the bottle in my toiletry bag. I look at myself in the mirror until it's fogged up and I jump into the shower. I lather up my hair with shampoo. The lozenge is half melted in my mouth, and I keep my mouth shut tightly. The steam enters my lungs and fills them to capacity. I feel it swirl and realize how small my lungs are now. I let the air out and find myself wanting it back, wanting more of it. I sit down in the tub, my head between my knees, and let the hot water overrun me.

After several minutes, I get up and turn off the shower. I towel myself dry and put on my old clothes. I dash out of the bathroom and pick up my jacket and phone.

"I'll be right back," I tell them, with my back to them already, halfway out the door.

"Where are you going?" Mom says behind me. "Your hair is all wet. You'll catch a cold."

"Hi, it's me."

"Hi, it's you. How's San Jose?"

"It's cold. It's chilly. It's overcast. I can see clouds billowing above me even though it's almost ten. It's like the mouth of hell. I think seasons are overrated."

"You sound bad. You have that sexy voice like when people are about to get sick."

He tries to be funny, but I don't laugh. "I don't feel sexy, which is a good thing. My sister-in-law already thinks I'd be climbing over my grandma in bed."

"That's disgusting. You're sharing a bed with your grandmother?"

"And sharing a room with my parents."

"Really?"

"Shut up."

"Okay. Why did you call then?"

"To hear your voice. Any voice but that of anyone I'm with right now. I just want to tell someone I don't want to grow old. Old people are slow, and they forget things. Old people are old. I don't want to grow old alone."

"We can move in together."

"That's a terrible idea. We've only been dating for three months."

"But I love you." He says it without any irony.

"Well, about that. One dinner with my family would cure that."

"No, it really won't, Mason." I like the joking boyfriend better.

"Besides, another new person in my grandmother's life would confuse her even more."

"She can't be confused with me. How many Black guys does she know?"

"You're Black? Really, you're not, are you?"

"Ah, I knew that would be a problem for her."

"She's ninety-four. Not sleeping in her own bed is a problem for her."

"Your grandmother is ninety-four? How old are you really?"

"That's the other reason why we can't move in. You'll leave me for a younger man sooner or later."

"Just exactly how young would that younger man have to be to be younger than you?"

I start crying. I don't know why. He is what I want.

"I can drive up to San Jose right now," he coos, at the right moment. "Tell me where you are. We can get our own room."

I don't tell him no yet. I just want to savor that possibility longer.

He asks, "Why do you go along with everything they say? You don't have to, you know?"

"I don't know why." But I do. I go along with it for the same reason I just told him I didn't know why. It takes too much to explain to someone in your world about another world that you also live in. Sometimes it's just easier to go along.

He asks again to come up and see me. He could be here by three in the morning if he left this moment. I could get a room now. We could have several hours together, and he could tell me jokes that I could retell in my head during the wedding. I would smile at nothing like an idiot all through the banquet and nobody would know why. He could wait for me in the room until all the pomp and circumstance is over. When I don't say yes to any of his proposals, he asks, "How can you turn down hotel sex?"

I force myself to laugh to make him feel better, but it comes out like a snicker. "No, I feel better now. Thanks." As soon as I said that, the crying made sense: it was what I came out here to do, away from them.

When I go back to the hotel room, it is dark and quiet. I go into the bathroom and take another swig of that cough syrup. I change into my pajamas. Without turning on the lights, I slide under the covers. I sleep, with my back to Grandma and a gulf between us. I can tell them I have a cold, and I need to have my own room. But that's just too much explaining now and nagging later. It's just easier to hide a cold.

My mother starts snoring.

"What's that noise?"

I turn and when my eyes adjust to the dark, I can see Grandma's eyes, wide open.

"It's just Mom," I tell her.

Someone farts from the other side of the room.

"And that's probably Dad."

"When are we leaving? I can't stay here."

"Why can't you stay here?"

"Because this is not my home. I need to go back to Taiwan."

"You don't live in Taiwan. You live in Los Angeles with Mom and Dad."

"Los Angeles?"

"Remember, we drove up here."

"Yes, and we have to return the car. How are we going to get home?"

"No, it's not a rental. We'll take you home."

"I'm worried."

"Why?"

"I worry your father doesn't have enough money. I worry about my third son. I haven't heard from him in a long time. It's very hard to be a parent."

"Dad is retired. They have enough to live on. And Uncle is fine." Uncle passed away almost ten years ago. "Go to sleep. You're going to a wedding tomorrow, and we're going home the day after. Say it yourself. You'll remember better."

She says exactly what I told her. Then she asks me, "What's that noise?"

"That's Mom snoring."

"Is she going to snore all night?"

"Probably." I smile. "She's tired."

I touch her on her shoulder. Her flesh feels soft and loose under her clothes. Jesus, am I trying to infect her? But she won't catch a cold. I know she won't. She'll live another ten years, easy. And more and more—that scares me more than it pleases me.

I can finally feel the cough syrup working now. "The lady stole the immortality potion from her archer husband and escaped to the moon."

She says, "I think you're right."

"Her name is Chang'e. I'll tell you the story another night. You don't have to worry when I'm here," I tell her. "I'll take care of you. I'll take you home."

"You're really my favorite grandson," she says.

I smile. Then I ask her, "Who am I, Grandma?"

"You're David."

"That's right, Grandma. Go to sleep." I close my eyes but do not turn away. So if she wakes up in the middle of the night, it won't be a stranger's back she faces, and she'll know she's safe. I take my hand off her shoulder and pull the blanket over my shoulder. I shrink beneath it, just enough so she can't feel my breath.

TWELVE STEPS

"My therapist doesn't think I'm capable of falling in love," I say as I get out of the car from the passenger's side. I say it because I don't want what's-his-name—Chris? Curtis?—to think that this is more than what it is. He's been quiet in the car, I think, because I was asking all these questions about him. But they were for security reasons only. I don't really want to know him.

He's walking in the opposite direction he drove in and leads the way. "My apartment is down the street quite a bit. Parking sucks here."

"You don't have to tell me. I used to live in Belmont Shore."

He doesn't look back when I speak. So I just look at his back. Hunched forward, his shoulders bulge as if wings had been clipped from them.

"Are you cold?" I ask.

"So you're seeing a therapist?"

"I'm not crazy."

He turns around enough for me to see a square inch of his cheek: he's smiling. "Didn't say you were."

"I don't have to see him, just so you know."

"Then why do you do it?"

"Just cuz," I reply quickly. "Hey, how much farther are we?"

"Don't change the subject," he snaps but points down the street for me, anyway. "I told you I had to park far."

"This house is for sale. How much do you think it goes for?"

"You're doing it again. Maybe if you save up the money from the therapist you don't need, you can afford to move back to this neighborhood." He turns, again to smile.

"You know, your head turns left. Are you left-handed? Cuz most people turn to the right." I use the opportunity to put my hand on the back of his neck. "Here, turn around now."

He shakes my hand off. Now he puts his hands in his pockets like a paranoid turtle. "Hey, bro, are you having a manic episode, or do you always talk this much? Maybe you've got too much brain in you and not enough space in your head to hold it in."

I catch up to him to check out his face, making sure I haven't gone too far. I've worked on him all night; I'm getting so close, and I don't want to blow it half a block—or however far away—from his apartment. He has a blank expression that I can't read. I jump ahead and face him, walking backward.

"Do you know where you're going, brain boy?" he asks.

I shrug. He is not good-looking, but I don't need a leading man. Every time I fuck one of those, I feel like I'm in a porn video. His face is so fleshy that it can wear more than one emotion at a time. In the club, it was the seriousness in his eyes that caught my attention. Now, there's mischief in his cheekbone, balancing on his restrained mouth: he's not mad. He also has a strong jaw. His skin is tough but clean. No, he's not a leading man, but he has a great bone structure and his face improves on it.

"I go to the community clinic by the Diagonal," I say.

"What?" His eyes slope very slightly toward the bridge of his nose. There is a little fire in them.

"My therapist. That's where I see my therapist. Every other week. They have a sliding scale. That's how I afford it."

"Well, keep sliding your crazy, backward-walking, punk ass, cuz no one who lives in these houses pays for discount therapy."

"Do you enjoy talking to me that way?"

"Either get the hell out of my way or shuffle your feet faster. It's cold out here."

"Cuz you have a hard-on."

"You're crazy. And you're a liar, too, cuz you *do* clearly need a therapist."

"But you do have a hard-on. It wasn't that big in the club before." I point at it, but he doesn't follow my finger.

"Shut the fuck up."

"Tell me, Jack," he says patiently. This is going to be one of those "processes," I can tell. He's going to take me through a process where his brilliant sequencing of questions would elicit answers that reveal the faulty logic behind my action and thereby get me to own my problems. "Tell me," he repeats. "What do you think my job is here?"

He knows I'm immune to this shit. I've told him my parents used to reason with me when I was just learning how to speak. They didn't believe in spanking. They thought that every child, from the age of four, has the capacity to reason, and that if you treat him like an adult, he will act like one. Whatever that means.

I think about his questions. Then I reply confidently, "To help me."

"Yes?" He nods and wants more.

"To challenge me?"

"Well, I don't want you to do anything you're not ready for. But yes, I do want you to be able to examine your life, to break out of a comfort zone that doesn't serve you anymore."

"Or accept it."

"Well, if you have to."

"I understand."

"Do you? Do you, really? Because you insist on telling me these stories that are not true . . ."

"You mean lies?"

"Exaggerations, maybe. Lies, I don't know. But do you know why you're telling me these things?"

"But they are true."

He leans forward, casting aside his notepad. He has stopped writing on it fifteen minutes into the session. He begins, "You're telling me that the guy you went home with had a roommate, and the three of you had a ménage à trois."

"Well, not exactly. It wasn't really a roommate. It was a friend who was crashing on his couch for a couple weeks. He was sleeping in the living room when we started. And we didn't have a ménage à trois as much as they took turns screwing me. I really don't think they wanted to be together. The second guy left the room as soon as he was done. The first guy and I fooled around some more, and then he took me home."

"That didn't happen!"

"I swear we didn't have a threesome."

"No, I mean the whole thing. It's something out of your fantasy."

"I'm not delusional, Mr. Rodriguez. I know a delusional person would say the same thing, with just as much conviction, but I'm not delusional."

"I don't think you are at all."

"And I didn't say it to shock you."

"It's interesting that you said that. But actually I think there's more truth in that statement than you yourself believe."

I throw my hands up.

Ignoring me, he continues, "And let me tell you. I might not have done this as long as someone else. But I'm not as young as I look. I've heard enough whacked-out things in this world for two lifetimes. I don't shock easy. So I ask you again. Why, do you think, are you telling me these stories?"

"They aren't stories, and they aren't fantasies. Giving you a blow job while you're analyzing me is a fantasy. Cuz it's never going to happen. What I told you, happened."

Now he is silent. This is his other tactic: let me say enough words to replenish the ones that he's thrown back at me to no avail. To keep him going, I would do just that.

"I have to say. After so many months, I'm hurt by your lack of confidence in me."

He remains immobile. Not even a shrug or a raised brow. The words I gave have not filled up his cartridge. He's not ready to discharge yet. We're officially in a staring contest. A full minute passes by. I look beyond him. There's a window that looks out to the parking lot. They've cordoned off some of the lot to repair the surface. Two men in long-sleeved shirts are idling by a pickup truck, taking a break. It's a bright day outside. The room is dimming in my periphery. I feel as if I've fallen into a well and the window is the opening. And Mr. Rodriguez is looking down the well at me.

"You think I'm so fucked up that I would make something like that up? Would you like me more if I'm more fucked up?"

"Is that important to you that I like you?" He says the word *like* in an ugly way.

I pause and smirk. I turn my body a little sideways to hide my hard-on from thinking about giving him a blow job. I want to tell him, I've already gotten what I want out of this session. He can say whatever he wants.

"You think I enjoy discovering these problems in people," he says, his voice rising. "You think I talk about them at parties like they were my petulant children. You think talking to you every other week makes me feel better about myself. You have no idea. But even if you believe that I feel superior to the people I help, that's still not the reason you tell me these stories."

"I don't think you should go back to him," Jayne says. She stares at me intensely for two and a half seconds and then starts to giggle.

"He sounds unprofessional," Kat concurs.

"This staring thing is not happening. It's silly." Now she's trying it on Kat, who almost chokes when she receives the attention.

"Of course not," I rebut. "You're supposed to make contact, lock your eyes with the guy, and then gently look away. You're not supposed to stare him down like you're going to kill him and his family. Here, you try it, Kat."

Kat is the timid one among us, but she's had half a beer, so she's game. She shakes her body and gets ready. "Who should I try it on?"

"This place is dead."

"There was a cute guy on the other side of the bar when we walked in," Kat says.

I stand up and survey the room like a periscope to get a clearer view of the room on the other side of the bar. I can't see the guy Kat is talking about. There is a guy sitting at the midpoint of the bar, nursing his drink. The only other person sits closer to us, working on the day's crossword puzzle, with half a burger on his plate.

"Sit down," they both exclaim.

"No one cares. And besides, you're supposed to be a little obvious. Guys need encouragement."

"Did he really say you can't be in love?" Kat asks.

Jayne corrects her. "'You are incapable of falling in love.' That's what he said, right? Therapists are like that. Either you can't love, or you're falling in love with them, so they can say you're projecting and therefore something is wrong with you."

"Why the hell did you pick this table? The one cute guy is on the other side." I ask Kat.

Jayne says, "I know which one you're talking about." She sits back, completely in her element though it's her first time here. She has a model's slenderness, and there's a way she flings her silky black hair that will intimidate less confident men. Kat is the opposite. She's a little thick at the waist, and she knows it. What she doesn't realize is that her large breasts make everything proportional. She could even be voluptuous if she showed more of her body. But her self-consciousness is appealing; it makes those men whom Jayne scares away comfortable. The two of them are a good team.

"I can't see him from here." The restrooms are on that side of the bar. So I tell them, "I'm going to the men's room."

"It doesn't matter," Jayne says with authority. "It's a Wednesday night. We're not going to pick up anyone tonight. No one's here."

"We're here."

"We wouldn't be here if we weren't trying out your stupid staring theory."

"Eye contact theory," I correct her. "I'm checking out the other side."

I stand up, leaving the two girls there. The bartender gives me a nod as he inverts a gin bottle on a thick little glass with one hand and sprays tonic in it with another. I know him from coming in here many times before. He's probably in his forties and has a potbelly and wavy brown hair, big, in the style of the seventies. He is kind of quiet for a bartender, like a vault of overheard secrets. There is a huge party a few tables away, three men and four women. None of the men stands out in the crowd.

I walk into the restroom and open the stall. It has both a toilet and a urinal, but no door between them. Just a protruding panel blocking the midsections of the bathroom users. A man pushes into the bathroom right after me. He's the guy who's been nursing the drink by himself at the bar. He is taller than I thought, and the bar top has hidden his brawn. He's built like a wrestler.

"Hey, bro," he says. "What's up?"

He looks at the arrangement and is taken aback, as I was, but goes straight for the urinal, anyway. Quickly getting over my displeasure, I resort to the toilet. He hovers very close to the urinal, as if he was about to be sucked down the drain. I start going, but there's no sound coming out from his side.

"Shhhhh, Shhhhh," I urge him along.

He turns a little to look at me, and I at him. I don't do it too defiantly, though. I just make enough eye contact to let him know that I'm not afraid of him. I think he's going to beat me up. I watched a nature show once that said that is what you're supposed to do when you encounter a bear: Don't show your fear. Keep your eye contact. Make wild and large gestures. I would make like I was drunk and fearless, too. Nobody wants to deal with a crazy drunkard.

Much to my surprise, he smiles. "What nationality are you?" he asks.

"Chinese."

"I'm Korean. You live around here?"

"I live a few blocks away. You?"

"I live in San Diego. I'm here for a convention." He sucks in. Finally, something is hitting the porcelain. "Drove out here to have dinner with a friend. I didn't want to go back to the hotel just yet." He returns his face to the wall. What a liar. The burger is his second dinner? Please. "Those are your friends you're with?" he asks.

I pull up my pants and flush. I cry, "Yeah." No more words exchanged as I wash my hands. As I make my way out, I say, "See you later."

"Yeah," he answers with his back to me.

When I get back to our booth, Jayne says, "That guy followed you to the restroom."

"Yeah, we saw him. He stood up almost right after you passed him and he followed you," Kat adds.

"He's kinda cute," Jayne says. Kat nods wholeheartedly.

"I know. He's Korean. He's from San Diego. He's in LA for business. And I guess he's staying at a hotel downtown somewhere."

They are impressed.

"And he's straight," I tell them.

"How do you know?"

I act annoyed. "I know."

"How?"

"He called me 'bro.'"

"That doesn't mean anything," Kat says. She doesn't believe there is any rule about flirting and dating and romance and relationships. She is why we are here. I think she needs a lesson about these things.

"Yeah, I think Kat is right. He's looking over here."

I turn around, and just as quickly, Kat tells me not to. He's back at the bar. I catch him looking at us, and he looks away.

"I think he's interested in one of you. He wasn't flirting with me in the restroom. The only thing he wanted to pump me for was information. Maybe he wants to find out if one of you is my girl."

"Let me try." With that, Jayne gets up and walks to the restroom on the other side like I had.

When she is out of sight, Kat starts on me. "Hey, Jack, I didn't want to say this in front of Jayne. I know she's trying to be supportive. We all want to help. But I don't think you should stop seeing the therapist. I'm so afraid you're going to go back to . . ."

"I'm not going back to him."

"And the sleeping around, that's not good either. That's not going to help any. Therapy will work. It takes time, but it'll work. You have to be open to it."

"No, Kat, I don't. I didn't end a relationship because I stopped loving him. I ended it to save him, and myself. But mostly him. I'm miserable without him, Kat. It's the most selfless act I've ever committed. It's like shooting your rickety, old-fogey dog." I can hear my voice escalating. "Fine, therapy takes time. I get that. But don't tell me I have to be open to therapy. I don't have to be open to anything for a long time."

Kat doesn't say anything. I think she's startled by my volume. I guess it not only works on bears in the wild.

"If people want to help, fine. But don't expect me to make it easy for them, so they can feel they're being helpful. I have no more sacrifices in me."

Kat turns away. I know she is hurt. A year ago, I would've apologized for my tone. But now I don't care. We stay silent until Jayne gets back.

"Well, he's definitely not interested in me. He didn't even turn his head when I passed by . . . twice!"

"Here, Kat, next time he looks this way, use my eye contact theory on him."

"No," she protests. She's mad at me.

"I think we've scared him, Jack," Jayne says. "He's not looking this way anymore."

"He will. Come on, Kat."

"No. Why can't Jayne do it? She thinks he's cute."

"Leave me out of it."

Flustered, Kat says to me, "I still think he's interested in you."

"You want me to prove it?"

"No, I'm afraid what you're going to do."

"I'm just going to order us a second round, that's all."

I stand up and leave the booth again. I can hear Kat shrieking behind me. I walk to the bar and plant myself behind the Korean guy and order three more beers from the bartender. He keeps looking at the side, and not at me. His fingers tap the bar top like legs of a nervous spider. I leave a twenty-dollar bill for the bartender and gather up the sweating bottles by their necks. Calmly, I walk back to the booth.

"See."

"See what?" Kat says.

"He doesn't even acknowledge me. It's not me he wants."

"You're standing behind him. You need to be in his field of vision."

"Now who's making up rules?" I snap back. "And besides, he knew I was there."

"Hey, Jack," Jayne says, glaring at me. "Pipe down."

"No one cares, Jayne. This is a fucking bar."

She whispers with a mean look, "The guy next to us can hear every single word."

"He's here all alone, so why don't we entertain him, too?" I mock-whisper. My voice is hoarse, and I keep it up. "I can go back and ask Mr. San Diego to join us. I can tell him, 'You're alone in a new town. Why don't I introduce you to my friends?'"

"No, I don't want him."

"Yes, you do. Why are you denying it?"

"Can we talk about something else? Like your therapist?" Jayne says.

"Oh, fuck my therapist. This is what I'm saying: The guy didn't have to pee but he followed me to the restroom to get information about one of you. He looked this way until I stared him down, Jayne-style. He's finished his drink for a while, and he's still here. There's no one else here on this side. He's away from home. I'm just saying he's a sure thing."

"Not anymore," Jayne says. "Some skank just sat next to him. They're talking now."

I turn around. It's one of the women from the big party on the other side. She has dark eye shadow, which contrasts with her light eyes.

"He's not into her," I say.

"How do you know?"

"Look at the way he's sitting. He's still sitting forward. If he's interested in her, he would've turned toward her."

"God," Kat screams. "No more rules. Not everyone plays these games. Why can't two people just talk and express how they feel about each other?"

"You think that's any better?"

"Let's just go," Jayne says. She's tired of it. She leaves us without waiting. We leave our drinks behind and follow her.

We are walking back to my place, where they've parked. We walk a block without saying anything. Then, out of nowhere, Kat sighs. "He was checking me out when we filed past him. The woman was still talking to him, but he looked away from her. I was at the door when I turned around. He saw me see him. He had this disappointed look."

"Oh, fuck you, Kat," I say.

Kat's eyes become red. "Why are you always picking on me?"

"If you can have something in your hand and you let it go, don't come to me for sympathy. You just don't do that."

"Jesus, Jack. Leave her alone." Jayne punches my shoulder. "She's not like you, okay. She doesn't pick up guys from a bar. Why can't you be more considerate and think about how you make her feel?"

"Me?" I yell. "What about how *she* makes me feel?"

"What? How do I make you feel?" Now there are tears.

"You can have something you want, but you turn it down. Fine. But you make me feel bad for wanting it."

"No, she doesn't," Jayne defends her.

"Yes, she does."

"No, I don't." She's choking on her tears. She coughs and sniffles alternately.

"Why can't I live closer?"

"Hello." He answers the phone with a heavy breath.

"It's me," I say.

There is a pause. So still is his side that I think we might have been disconnected. Finally, he says, "It's 2:30."

"Did I wake you?"

"No."

"So how are you doing?"

"Did you call here last week?"

"No." I lie.

"Yes, you did. You called. My mom answered and you pretended you called the wrong number and asked for Ed Begley III."

"The one time your mother gives you my message."

"It's so fucking you. You want to be caught."

"So how are you doing?"

"I've been sober for seven months, thank you very much."

"That's ironic. I just came back from a bar. A straight bar. And I almost picked up a guy, too." He says nothing. So I continue, "So the program is working. Isn't one of the steps where you have to call up people in your past and make amends with them?"

"Well, I'm not there yet. Is that what you're doing? Making amends? What's your program?"

"Apparently, sleeping around is my twelve-step."

"I don't want to hear that."

"I don't either. But that's what I do." Part of me wants to tell him I sleep with them and I leave them. But no matter how many times I do it, I'm not used to the leaving. I don't say that, after all, because I don't want him to hear it. With him I don't want to wear that armor of irreverence I do with my therapist or my friends.

"What does your therapist have to say about that? Are you still seeing a therapist?"

"A different one. He's cute, probably in his late twenties. He's kinda self-righteous, too. I like that. I get horny telling him the men I've been with. And he gets all worked up because he thinks I'm flouting his authority, like he's some father figure to me. It gets me more turned on. I go back every week for that. How about you? Are you seeing anyone?"

"Yeah, I have a therapist. Apparently I'm not as sick as you are, though."

"No. I mean, have you met anyone?"

"It's none of your business."

"Not even a rebound guy? You need a rebound guy to get over someone."

"I don't believe in that."

"I've been sleeping with thirty guys since we broke up. If I don't believe in that, I'd be a slut. Don't you need to screw someone else to get over me? Was I not worth even that to you?"

"We didn't break up. You left me," he corrects me. As if he could sense me sniffling, he adds quickly, "Hey, hey, you said I was killing you. And you know what? You were right about that. I was killing you. I wasn't about to do that to someone else. Part of me still thinks you should've stuck with me because I needed you then. But you were right about the killing part."

"I couldn't stay." My voice grows weaker. "I was just enabling you."

"That's bullshit. That's just your therapist talking. We could've found a way."

I did tell Mr. Rodriguez the story about how I had to take a dump in the bathroom with him passed out, curling around the porcelain. That's when I decided I needed to leave him. And I did. I pulled up my pants and took what I had to and disappeared. Mr. Rodriguez told me I did the right thing. It sounded odd because I didn't expect anyone to tell me that was the right thing to do, but that's what everyone said. "I was drinking with you. Don't you remember? We're both in a better place now."

"Oh, I disagree. You called here, Jack, and pretended you were looking for someone else when my mom answered the phone. And you called again tonight, at two in the morning, obviously desperate, telling me that you've been sleeping around. And I'm so pathetic that I'm actually talking to you at two fucking o'clock in the morning. You, who left me foaming at the mouth on the bathroom floor. I'm so pathetic that I think if I keep you on the line long enough, you'll take me back. So I ask you, Jack, is either one of us that much better off now than when we were together?"

"Sadly yes."

"What are you doing calling me, Jack?"

"I don't know."

"You want me to come over?"

"Yeah, right." I chuckle. I do want him to come over. It's all I want. If I had that, I would want nothing else. "You'll stumble back to step one. And I'll have to sleep with another thirty guys."

"Come back to me."

I think about it for a moment. I can't believe I'm thinking about it. "I can't." I start sobbing when I realize he's serious and I have to be the strong one to tell him no, to shoot an old dog all over again.

"I'm better now. Didn't you hear me? I've been sober for seven months." Then, he coos to my sobbing, "Come back. Daddy'll take care of you."

"No."

"C'mon, baby. Daddy needs you. He's been working so hard so he can take care of you. Daddy loves you. He wants to come home." The phone cannot distort his voice. It's exactly like it was when he used to whisper in my ear, the way I remember it. "You have something for your Daddy when he comes home, don't you?"

"Please stop."

He takes a deep breath, heavier than the one he answered the phone with. "Then stop calling me, you selfish bastard."

"I'm sorry. I should go."

"What did you think you were going to accomplish tonight?"

"I don't know. I just wanted to hear . . ."

"Do you know what your voice is doing to my nerves right now?" He coughs.

"You're right. I shouldn't have called you." I'm trying to control my sobbing and settle my breaths. "I should go," I say, though I don't hang up.

"Don't." He becomes gentle again. "Stay on for a little while more. So thirty guys, huh?"

I laugh.

"Don't hang up," he says. "We don't have to talk. Please. Let me hear you cry."

A BOY NAMED SUE

I was supposed to be a boy.

I am the youngest of four, another daughter after already three. Before I came along, my family had already moved out of the overcrowded apartment in Chinatown. The economy was doing better, if only because both my parents had steady jobs. Three steady jobs, to be exact, between the two of them. Plus some odd ones here and there. They found a house for rent in Highland Park, a four-bedroom at the corner of Marmion and Joy. Small bedrooms, but there were four, enough for each of my sisters to have their own room. Still close to Chinatown—it wasn't Alhambra or Rosemead, where our better-off relatives began to settle, but far enough from those warrens hidden behind restaurants and factories and village associations. Wider streets. More distance from the freeway. A stand-alone house. Practically a suburb those days. They were feeling optimistic. So Pop wanted to try one more time, for a boy.

Their luck ended there.

He named me Susan.

A year later, my mother fell ill and quickly died of a respiratory-related illness that her friends insisted she got from working in a garment factory.

Their luck was fucked.

In spite of all that, I had a happy childhood. Pop was overworked, so we could afford to stay in that house. Oldest Sister worked part time, too, at the McDonald's on Figueroa. She got the cooks to make extra burgers right before they closed that they were supposed to throw away at the end of their shift. That was our breakfast the next day. Second Sister took care of me. She was all of thirteen when Mother died. I got to wear boys' clothes, hand-me-downs from my cousins in the San Gabriel Valley because they were closer in age to me than Third Sister. I cut my hair when my neck could feel it. But I never did a good job. Second Sister would fix it, and making it worse, she just shaved it all off. I rode my secondhand bike down the street in any of those Little League jerseys from my cousins' discard pile, and the Chinese people in the neighborhood would call me Child Monk. When the boys played baseball in the street, I chased down the errant balls that they couldn't catch and threw them back as hard as I could.

Needling the younger boys, their captain would say, "Get ready, Sue. I'm going to hit it so far that none of them can run it down."

They loved me.

I was supposed to be a boy.

I was a boy.

By the time Pop finally noticed me, it was too late. I was sixteen. I had made out with a girl, a cheerleader and a senior, no less. She didn't get in trouble but I did. My father screamed, face-slapped me, and then yelled some more. When none of that produced the remorse he sought, he kicked me out of the house. Which is fine. I didn't want to go back to that school, anyway. The boyfriend was probably going to get his friends to beat me up. This time, I had given them a legit excuse.

Since his early seventies, Pop has developed early onset of Alzheimer's. Second Sister takes care of him, in the same house. She gets some government money for in-home care, and her husband is a teacher in Artesia. They have a ten-year-old son. Sometimes, they sublet the extra room to a boarder, always someone new to the country just trying to get their sea legs.

The landlord has always liked us. Every other summer, he shows up in person, with baked goods from a local panaderia, and asks how the old man is doing in this heat without any air-conditioning, before he apologetically tells Second Sister that he has to raise their rent by 3 percent. But this year, he showed up to tell them he was getting out of the rental market. The time was right. He was going to sell the house. They should get ready.

Second Sister called to tell me they are packing. If I want anything, I have to claim it now.

That's about as solid an invitation as I'll ever get.

I don't think Pop recognizes me. He eyes me like a stranger and goes back to his television. I don't know if it's Alzheimer's, or if it's me. I just nod at him silently. Maybe I don't want him to recognize me.

My nephew looks up from his homework and greets me with "Uncle Sue." I met him only two years ago, but for some strange reason he has taken a liking to me. That first time we met, he asked why I had a funny name, a girl's name. I answered with a question: "Do you know the song 'A Boy Named Sue'?" He shook his head. "It was a Johnny Cash song. I bet you don't know who he is either." He shook his head again, conspicuously losing his patience.

"There was this boy named Sue. Obviously. His father named him that and then he disappeared from his life. People would pick on him because of his name. He had no one, so he had to fend for himself. He started picking fights everywhere. One time, he ran into his old dad, and they got so bloody fighting each other." And here, Nephew cracked a smile. I got him hooked. "And when they were out of breath, the father explained he had to name him Sue because he was a wanderer, a rolling stone, and he knew he would never be around, and his son had to toughen up for himself."

I hadn't kept my given name out of respect for the man who gave it to me. I kept it for Johnny. It made me feel tougher.

I pet Nephew on his head and ask him what he's working on. He says he's writing a story. Again. Because Second Sister didn't like the first one.

"He wrote about his grandpa going to the bathroom leaving the door open," she explains. "It's true. It doesn't mean I want the whole world to know. He's peed in the backyard once. I keep the back door locked now. It was so hot during summer."

My nephew chimes in, "In American concentration camps, they only put partitions between every other toilet."

Second Sister explains, "Some field trip to the Japanese American National Museum. It's how he got his idea for the first story."

"The women could talk to each other while they took a shit." He blithely relishes the last word.

My sister and I both exclaim, "Hey, hey, hey."

Suddenly he turns somber, "It's inhuman."

I want to correct him. *Inhumane.* But he's not wrong.

I ask my sister if they have found a new place.

"We just put in an application for an apartment in Downey last weekend." At least it would be an easier commute for Brother-in-law. She continues, "Smaller than this place but not cheaper. It's already been tough. Now I expect all of you to chip in."

She eyes me sharply. Being kicked out is no exemption.

"I didn't know money's been tight."

"You could've asked."

I couldn't have helped much, anyway. I've spent my savings on hormone therapy, mastectomy, hysterectomy. And I'm not done.

She continues, "Money is one thing. It's so hard to move out of a house you've lived in all your life. You have no idea."

"Are you serious now?" I have plenty of ideas.

Quickly she retorts, "You have to forgive him." It's as if she's been waiting for the moment to say it. When I don't say anything in return, she says she's sorry.

After our talk, I go to the vacant boarder's room, my old room. In a desk drawer, I find a series of proof sheets. I yell for my sister. She comes right away.

"What's the matter?"

"I think this is yours."

"Hold on." She leaves the room only to return with a magnifying glass. A long time ago, she took up photography after a photojournalism class at LACC. She examines each frame on the first proof sheet. "Yes, I took these," she says, astounded.

"Who else could it be?" Oldest Sister had bought her a Kodak that was even older than me.

She moves over and down with the magnifying glass like a snake. Then she hands me the magnifying glass. "But look who this is."

I dive into the picture where she's stopped. A boy was running down the pavement with a kite behind him, trying to get it to soar. His back to the camera, oblivious. I could tell it was the end of our block. He was in the moment. He owned the street.

The boy was me.

I move down the proof sheet. Same shot, in consecutive moments. I was in motion. The kite rose, up, up, until eight, nine frames later, it disappeared.

It's slowly coming back to me. The perfect lawn belonged to our neighbors, a gay couple: one Asian, one white. Double income, a long line of equity, and no kids, unless you consider their Pomeranian. They say the gays come first, and make the neighborhood tidy and safe for everyone else. Guess it's true. At least for the gays, not for trans people like me.

I ask, "Remember that couple next door who kept complaining about our fence? And they just gave up and eventually put up their own fence? What happened to them?"

"Them? They sold as soon as we bounced back from the recession. They made a bundle. I think they're living in one of those townhouses in Chinatown now."

We both rolled our eyes at the same time, a small moment of solidarity. I'm definitely keeping these.

I say, "You were very good at it. What happened?"

"Cell phones," she says casually.

But I know the truth. *We* happened. We all left her with our father, voluntarily or not.

I offer to buy dinner when Brother-in-law comes home from work. I stroll down to Fidel's to pick up a pizza. At least Fidel's is still around.

After dinner, I offer to stay overnight and to keep helping her sort things the next day. She's right. It is harder than I thought to leave the house.

After midnight, I hear Pop holler from his room. "Hey, hey." The second longer than the first. To no one. Or to anyone. I get out of bed and fumble in the dark, hushed hallway toward his call. In his room, I crouch down to his bed and ask, "Are you okay?" Why is my voice an octave lower?

"Where am I?" he asks.

"This is your house."

"Where is the bathroom?"

"I'll take you." I heft him. The soft blanket rolls off him easily. I guide his arm behind my neck and lift him with my back. The same pajamas all these years. Their frayed edges chafe the back of my neck. I walk him to the bathroom.

"Do you need help?"

He shakes his head, like he's heard the question before. He pulls his pants down in front of me and sits on the toilet, letting out a breath as if our walk has exhausted him. I close the door, but not all the way. I hear him peeing. Through the crack, I see him rub his hands the way arthritic people do. He stands and hitches up his pajamas. He doesn't flush but remembers to wash his hands. I wait patiently on the other side of the door. When he comes out, he grasps my arm and we make the same trek back to his room.

I pull the blanket over his shoulders.

He asks me, "Who are you?"

I pull it snug, a temporary delay, a summon of courage. "I'm your son."

"My son?"

"Yes."

Satisfied with my assurance, he closes his eyes. The night takes him again.

DADDY ISSUES

1.

The sixth time I stayed over at Bruce's, he remarked that one of my nipples was bigger than the other. The sixth time, in the six months we had been together, he noticed. Not grotesquely bigger. Imperceptibly, even, he said, unless you were, well, intimate with it. It was three in the morning, during one of our postcoital talks. He had his sleeveless Iron Maiden shirt back on, his elbow propped on the pillow. I liked these talks. They were sexy and playful. New discoveries about our aging bodies, after a whole month without seeing each other. Just before he talked about my nipples, I had told him that I usually hated hairy chests, but I liked rubbing my cheek against his. His chest hair was not baby soft, just enough of the bristling. He said he had never had conversations like these with a hookup *after* sex. Neither had I.

"Which one?" I asked. Then I, betraying the fact that I already knew, said quickly, "It's not bigger."

"A-ha," he laughed, catching my slip.

"It just sticks out a little more," I corrected him. I was lying on my back, exposed and a little dirty. I might have dozed off when Bruce was in the shower. "It's my slutty nipple."

"Slutty nipple," he repeated fondly. He touched my right nipple. "This one is a good school boy." And then twisted the other one, "This is the slut. My slutty nipple."

I shrieked and he got on top of me to lick what he had hurt. Then he moved up to kiss my mouth. We were good kissers. I had my hand between his shirt and me. The cloth was thick, though the graphic on it was worn like chipped paint. The more he stuck his tongue inside my mouth, the more I pawed the shirt to feel his chest hair underneath it.

Bruce fancied himself a Daddy. Not the well-groomed, Titan-of-the-industry kind. And he didn't earn his thick upper arms by spending a few hours a day in a gym doing reps and wrestling with machines. He'd been in a rock band in his twenties and rode a Harley most of his adult life. Then he got into sound engineering when he realized there were way better bassists than he. He had even set up his own company and traveled all over the country and the Middle East, making a shitload of money. He hadn't told me what happened to that company, but seven years ago he started driving buses for Metro, until six months into the pandemic, when he got on disability. Not very Daddy-like, but in bed, I mangled different parts of his bio and imagined him a roadie that I had to sleep with in order to get a backstage pass after a Limp Bizkit concert. The boys he fucked around with were probably not into hard rock. But I wasn't a twink anymore. Our age difference could be accounted for with one hand. With his handlebar mustache, he looked like Sam Elliott twenty years ago, and I was what Bowen Yang would look like in ten years. He wasn't my type, nor was I his. But we both knew there were plenty of muscle band shirts where the one he was wearing came from that he would never wear around those boys.

Months ago, the second time we'd hooked up, I did something with Bruce that I had never done with a fuck buddy. Since my breakup just before the pandemic, I hadn't stayed the night at anyone's. Not only did I stay the night at Bruce's that time, but I hung out and ran errands with him the next day. Daddy's truck had been stolen and was recovered a few days before, but he had missed the registration deadline. We went to the DMV to see if we could get the late fees waived. After waiting for an hour, he found out he needed to get a police report from the California Highway Patrol. When he asked the woman behind the counter where the closest CHP office was, she shrugged and wordlessly pointed to his phone. Bruce was incredibly patient with bureaucracy. He just closed his thin manila folder and thanked the DMV employee for her time. Even smiled and called her ma'am.

I liked seeing that gentlemanly side of Bruce. It was like bring-your-child-to-work day at Daddy's office, where you get to see him interacting with other adults. Or I imagined so, since my own daddy had worked as a driver for the California lottery, and had sold home alarm systems door to door before that. In Hong Kong he had been a teacher.

I looked up the closest CHP office on my phone and was navigating for him. Between turns, Bruce got talkative. The first guy he ever fooled around with was his stepfather. He was barely a teenager. It was all hand jobs and blow jobs. His mother must have found out because that was around the same time she became verbally abusive to him. And soon his older sister got into the act, too, calling him faggot loser, worthless piece of shit, zero. He had run away when he was sixteen and had become homeless for a stretch. At this point of the story, he took his eyes off the road and gave me a knowing look on the side. He wasn't about to tell me what he did to survive living on the street, but he definitely wanted me to imagine it. I smiled and nodded and reminded him to make a left at the next intersection.

"When I was making six figures, I thought they would be proud of me," he said. "But you know what my sister said? She said I was going to blow all of it sooner or later. Self-fucking-fulfilling prophecy."

I sidled up to him in his roomy cab and put my hand on his knee. I appreciated the vulnerability, but I also wanted him to stop. It was only our second time together. He cupped my hand with his. My message not received.

Just then, his phone rang, and he picked it up through his truck's Bluetooth. Some dude asked him where he was and when he could help him move. He had to get out of his place by the end of the day.

Bruce said, "I don't know if I could, man. I'm running an errand right now."

"Please," the dude pleaded. The way he said it, I could tell they had fucked before. I could also tell Bruce didn't want to, but he asked, "How many boxes do you have?"

"Just a few. C'mon, please." He extended the last word even longer than the last time.

I shook my head vigorously to give him permission to say no. For good measure, I squeezed his knee.

He said, "Let me try to figure something out and call you back."

After he hung up, I asked, "Who's this guy?"

Bruce didn't answer me at first.

"He's one of your sons, isn't he?"

"Damian and I don't fuck anymore. We haven't fucked in months."

"It's okay. I don't do monogamy." We had laid out the ground rules a few days ago when we decided to meet again after our first time. I had told him that I would see him no more than once a month. At my age, I was looking for quality, not frequency. Between hookups, he could do whatever he wanted. He agreed, no expectations. "The only expectation," I had added, "is that when we are together, it's just the two of us. Just like last time."

In the truck, with my hand still on his knee, he was actually calculating how he could finish his errands and help out this guy.

I asked, "Did you promise him that you were going to help him move today?"

"No."

"So he just called last minute and expected you to show up."

"Damian calls when Damian needs something."

Oh, boy, I thought. This has happened before.

Bruce continued, "I could pick him up after CHP. He said he'd have only a few boxes. I could drop him off on my way to the DMV . . ."

"I think you should focus on your errands. It's already Friday and you only have a few hours left. I'm sure he's pretty resourceful." When Bruce didn't answer me, I said, "Why don't we just go to the CHP first and see how long that takes? You can make a decision then."

He nodded.

At the CHP, while he was waiting in line, I went over to the In-N-Out down the block and got us lunch. He was still in line when I got back. He told me I didn't have to stand with him, so I gave him his iced tea and went to one of those plastic chairs and ate my burger.

It took almost an hour to get the report. It was almost three when Bruce was finally eating his lunch in his truck.

"You got me an iced tea," he said.

"I got you lunch."

"But you got me an iced tea because you saw I have a bunch of Snapple iced teas in my fridge and you knew I like it."

I nodded.

"You're very good to me," he said.

"It's just iced tea." I was touched that he was grateful for such small things.

"Damian has been calling but I let it go to voicemail."

"I'm proud of you."

He took a big bite out of the In-N-Out. I unzipped his jeans, pulled his dick out, and sucked it.

Two days later, he called to say thank you. Not just for the sex. He said, "Damian called. He ended up finding someone else to help him." (*Of course he did*, I thought to myself.) Then he told me how he had met Damian online more than a year ago. The guy tricked him into picking him up from a rehab on the Westside. Bruce swore they had fucked just once. Damian had since moved on to other men, he said. More generous ones. But he still called Bruce once in a while if he needed something. I could imagine Damian even though Bruce didn't describe him: young (barely legal), exquisite, entitled. Becky with the good hair she didn't need to pay for.

"Why would you keep someone like that in your life?" I asked.

"I can't help it. People need help, and I'm in a position to help them."

I thought, obviously, the kind of help Damian ultimately wanted was not something Bruce could give. Money was one thing Bruce didn't have a generous supply of. I also thought it was all that trying to please his family, who couldn't be pleased. But all I said was, "You're such a Daddy."

Bruce continued, "Anyway, thank you. I don't think I could've gotten all that shit done without you."

2.

I know why one nipple is sluttier than the other. I regret telling my ex because he stopped touching it after I told him. He stopped being playful altogether. Back when I was using, in my twenties and thirties (before I met my ex), I'd stay up for hours watching porn and jerking off when I was high. Most of the time I couldn't get hard. I had a sliver of a chance if I played with my nipple and I masturbated with my left hand. I used my nondominant hand so I could pretend someone else was doing it. So my right hand touched my left nipple. For hours. Sometimes my skin was so dry and I didn't realize it. Even when it broke skin, I kept going. I imagined all the bad things that I had let men do to me, and then wanting to go back for more, for worse. I was that high. I was that out of control.

I knew how much my ex hated that story, or any story from that time in my life. I had gotten through it, and he thought we didn't have to talk about it anymore. Even when I tried to cover my slutty nipple for my ex, it poked out when I wore a T-shirt too tight. But I had gotten through those dark times—it wasn't nothing; it was the point.

Six years into our relationship, I quit my job (to my ex's chagrin) and focused on my art. I used to think I could have a nine-to-five and paint on the side. In college, I had taken art classes only after I was done with the requirements for my economics degree. After I graduated, I went to a local community college and took a class on form and space, and another one on wheel throwing, just because I had thought I wanted to use my hands more. I signed up for an etching class the third semester, but I skipped most of those classes because I got a promotion at work. I didn't even bring my easel and art supplies with me when I moved two years later. To take a class on acrylic painting again, this time with a dozen people half my age, was both the most humbling and most exciting thing that had happened to me during my relationship.

For my final project for that class, I did a self-portrait on the slutty nipple. There was some cubist influence—my torso was lopsided, the left side encroaching on the viewer. I was proud of my color choices to reveal depth. I played with texture and even got the paint to bubble at the tip of the nipple. It got picked for the student show that the department put together at the end of the school year. I invited my ex and all our friends.

The next day, my ex broke up with me. The conversation went something like this:

You have all the choices to paint different subjects. You painted that?

What did you think I was going to paint?

Landscape. Portrait.

It was a portrait.

Normal middle-aged people don't give up their job to pursue their dream to paint . . . what? Their deformed nipple?

That's a bit reductive.

I want someone to grow old with.

I want someone that I could still grow with.

Grow up. Get a job and grow the fuck up.

In the end, my ex realized that I had betrayed him, walked back on the stability that a monogamous relationship promised us in our adulting. He realized, too, that I wasn't going to change anytime soon. Once he said that out loud, that was the clarity I had needed to leave the relationship. The breakup was his bluff. I called him on it.

3.

The night Bruce discovered my slutty nipple, I told him, "Let's call them something else. Let's call them strawberries." He was sucking on the slutty one, getting hard again as the sun rose. "Why?" he stopped to ask. The effect was hot air on my stiff tip. I shivered and gripped his sheet. Then I laughed. "Did I just turn into my ex?" I said out loud. I told Bruce about his aversion to . . . my strawberries. In retelling it, I quickly realized it wasn't that. "The word is sacred," I said. "It's like we shouldn't just take its name in vain. That should be a commandment."

He stopped licking it to look at me and said, "Your stupid ex didn't want them; these are my boys now." Then he went to town on the other one.

We fucked again and then we slept for a few hours. When we woke up, it was almost two. Bruce asked me about my applying for graduate programs in fine arts. It was too soon to find out, I said. He asked to see the portfolio I submitted as part of my application. I had shown him the portfolio before. He'd thought I had excellent composition. I showed it to him on my tablet. He found the Slutty Nipple among the others and said he had always liked this one the most.

I stayed a second night. Bruce said if I wasn't going to come back for another month, it was the least I could do. Besides, it was our six-month anniversary. He cooked up ravioli that he had made and frozen a few nights ago and we dropped ecstasy after dinner. While waiting for it to hit, he dug up his acoustic guitar from the closet that he used to write music on. On his couch, he played with a few chord progressions, and then he found a melody. The guitar was like a barricade across his body that I couldn't find a way past. But I didn't mind not touching him for now. I could anticipate caressing him endlessly once we were rolling. Now my mind was just bathing in this scene that I was making up about fucking a rock god. He started mumbling some lyrics about making my schoolboy nipple slutty, too.

"What rhymes with slutty nipple?" he asked.

"Church steeple? Iced tea Snapple? Horny people?"

"It's easier to rhyme than strawberries for sure." He laughed and pulled my head to him. We started making out again, barricade be damned.

When we let go of each other, I said, "I don't think you can write a masterpiece about nipples."

"Hey, you should be proud of it. It's the mark of your sobriety. You made it out when so many didn't."

"It's not a big deal."

"Fifteen years of sobriety is a big deal."

"I mean, I wasn't an addict. I wasn't one of those a-taste-of-beer-and-I-fall-off-the-wagon types." When he rolled his eyes at me, I said, "Right, it's my mature beauty mark." I air-quoted "mature" and continued, "Other people get crow's feet. I have a slutty nipple."

He put his guitar away and pulled my shirt up. He kissed my slutty nipple and said, breathily, "Don't listen to him. You're perfect." Then he kissed my mouth and said he would finish that song before I came back next month. "You have to come back now," he said. There was a little insecurity in his voice. I asked him about the first guy he'd ever fallen in love with. We shared our sexual history, but we never talked about love. Another rule broken. Maybe the E was hitting me.

"Funny you should ask that," he said. "I got together with the person who turned out to be my first boyfriend because of E. I was in my thirties. Just got divorced from my wife and lost custody of my son because my shithead of a sister spread lies about me. So I was feeling depressed and this guy—he was one of my clients, he was producing a movie I was working on, he was related to the royal family in Saudi Arabia, too. He took me to a gay bar in WeHo—it was Arena. He said it would take my mind off my divorce because I would get a lot of attention. I was younger and didn't have a belly then."

"I like your belly," I said, rubbing my cheek on his belly to prove my point. Fuck, the E was hitting, and his body hair felt even better on my skin. It was like floating on a pillowy cloud with a thousand tiny massaging fingers.

"He gave me a pill. I didn't know it was E. And I was dancing with all these boys who were cuddling up to me, touching me. By the end of the night, he told me he had a crush on me. We kissed and I ended up at his place. That was it."

"Fuck me like you fucked him that night."

He let out a Daddy laugh.

"Fuck me like an Arabian princess." (Goddamn ecstasy!)

He swung his legs so I was fully on top of him, a textbook sixty-nine. Now I was flying. Bruce was my flying carpet. He buried his face in my ass. I could feel all the papillae on his tongue.

I called him after I got home the next morning and told him I had never stayed two nights in a row with anyone who was not a boyfriend, not even back when I was a binge drug user.

"That makes me feel special," he said. "So it won't be another month until I see you again?"

"If we do what we did the last two days, it might have to be longer. I'm older now. It takes a while to recover."

"I don't have to get high with you to have fun."

"Aww . . . that's like the nicest thing someone has ever said to me."

"It's not the E that makes you wild." He went on to describe the things I did, how I backed up on him, my muscle control "down there." He kept finding new nooks and crannies. I was guiding him without being a bossy bottom. He saw through my tricks.

Changing the subject, I asked, "Are you going to call your old boss today?" In one of our postcoital talks, he mentioned going back to Metro, maybe a desk job this time. I didn't ask about the specifics of the terms for his disability. He didn't want to go back driving. It wasn't just the sitting in the driver's seat all day. They gave him routes in some of the toughest neighborhoods in LA. It was wilder than any wild, wild west that Sam Elliott had ever faced.

"After I hang up with you, baby," he said. "And after I work on your song some more."

4.

By Tuesday morning, my body had recovered enough to drive up to Santa Paula. I got a gig with my professor working with some young people whose parents were farmworkers to paint a mural at a community center. It didn't pay much, but I could probably cover rent for about a week and a half. Now that I didn't live with my ex, and with my savings depleting, I had to rely on food stamps, Medi-Cal, and my best friend Essie's guest room. I knew I'd probably have to go back to waiting tables, like I had the last time I was in college. Or something similarly mindless that still offered quick cash. For now, I promised myself I'd only take on art or art-adjacent jobs.

On the way, Bruce texted me and asked how his boys were.

I pulled over to the side of the highway. I messaged him, "They don't listen to me anymore. They missed their daddy." That was another first. The flirty texts usually stopped by the second day. We'd leave each other alone until a few days before the one-month embargo expired.

"Even the schoolboy?" he texted back. Before I could think of a sexy response, he wrote he really wanted to see me again. "This weekend?"

I told him I was on my way to Ventura County and would work there until Sunday. "We're prepping the wall today & tomorrow. Thurs we'll scale the design the kids have come up with. Then they're going to come on Fri and Sat to paint the mural. We have a ceremony Sun after church. That's when most of their parents are free. And I promise my roommate I'll be at her party Sun night." I didn't know why I was sharing all those details in text.

"K," he texted back, "I'm proud of you, working artist. Take care of my boys."

I pulled up to a supermarket once I got into Santa Paula. My professor was staying at a Hampton Inn in the next town. His grant didn't account for accommodations for me, and he didn't offer to have me stay with him. Instead, he connected me with one of the high school students we'd be working with named Jasmine, and I was going to stay with her family closer to the community center. I thought I would bring some staples with me. Once I walked into the supermarket, I realized I had made a wrong choice. I had eschewed the big-chain stores in favor of what I had thought was a local market. This one looked like a warehouse and its exterior was unassuming. With a name of Fresas, what could go wrong? Inside, though, was all tidy, wood-beamed, and high-ceilinged. There was a whole wine section with a display of bottles lying about like they were just waiting to be packed in the crates they were propped up on. The next aisle had shelves of thirty different brands of sparkling water. I found the rice and beans that I had planned to get. The eggs were at least seven dollars a dozen, but I got three dozen, all courtesy of CalFresh. I got some avocados, limes, bananas, cilantro. All organic, because why not? I didn't know what kind of farmworkers Jasmine's parents were, but I'd figure they probably had some produce at home, maybe castoffs from work. The cheapest meat was the flank steak. I picked up a couple packets of that. They had a whole shelf of just tortillas—heirloom, sprouted whole grain, organic whole wheat, handmade white corn, cassava flour. I grabbed the Guerrero corn ones on the top shelf. Eighty count for a little over five bucks.

Jasmine's parents weren't home yet. She was tall for fifteen and had a healthy and even tan. When I arrived, she was helping her two younger sisters, twins, with their homework. I asked them what grade they were in, and they both shouted "THIRD" and stuck out three fingers to prove their point. They looked much smaller than their age, standing next to Jasmine, and their skin was fairer than hers. In the kitchen, I put my bag of groceries on top of the cooktop and took out one item at a time for Jasmine to stash away. She even got her sisters involved. They marveled at each like it was an ingredient they had not encountered before, even though there were already plenty of limes and avocados in the weaved basket on the counter. We made a good team. Then Jasmine, with her sisters in tow like ducklings, showed me their one-bedroom apartment. The bedroom, with one full-sized futon, belonged to her and her sisters, while her parents shared the pullout couch outside. As we walked back out, she mentioned that her mother would be staying in the room with them. When she talked, she pulled her long hair together behind her as if she was about to tie it into a ponytail, except she didn't have anything to tie it with, so she always ended up splaying it over her right shoulder. She pointed at the big couch. A pillow and a rather colorful quilt sat on one end. She said I could sleep there and her dad would take the floor. Her smile was big but apologetic. I said I couldn't. I had come with my own sleeping bag and was ready to take the floor. There was no way I could take the couch away from a farmworker. Jasmine said her mother wouldn't have it any other way, and I just had to take it up with her when she got home.

Around five, Jasmine started cooking dinner. She seasoned the steak and cooked the rice on the stovetop, since I was helpless without my Asian rice cooker. I made a lime-avocado dressing and soaked the beans for the next day. I took her sisters outside and started a fire for the grill. It was something Jasmine said she wouldn't be able to manage when it was just her holding down the fort. My family used to use charcoal once in a while to cook when we were little. My ex liked to grill, too, but he had a propane gas grill, one of those kinds with knobs and shelves on both sides that looked like an exploratory spacecraft had landed in his backyard. Not like the basic red round grill that Jasmine had with the sliding vent and something on the bottom to catch the ash.

At dinner, Jasmine had a lot of questions about Los Angeles. I said it wasn't all Hollywood and beaches. She wanted to know about celebrities. I gave up and said that I once waited tables on k.d. lang and another time on Drew Barrymore, who was as nice as she looked. And Bruno Kirby, before he died. He and his wife had a short conversation with me at the end of their meal on a slow night, and before they left, he shook my hand and told me his name as if I had not seen *When Harry Met Sally* a dozen times. She didn't know who those people were. I quickly rectified that by streaming *When Harry Met Sally* on my tablet for them after dinner. I told Jasmine that the best friend was Princess Leia. The twins still had no idea what we were talking about, but they laughed at the fake orgasm scene at Katz. I knew Jasmine got the joke, but the other two probably just thought Meg Ryan was funny screaming like that. For the rest of my stay, they would repeat "I'll have what she's having" to each other.

Jasmine was right. Her mother wouldn't let me sleep on the floor. I gathered that Jasmine had told her all the stuff I bought for their pantry while they were eating the meal she had cooked. Her mother told me, "You, el profesor." I kept saying, "No, soy estudiante." But either my Spanish was terrible or I just looked too old to be a student (or both). I slept on the couch while her husband took the floor.

I met my professor at the community center at ten the next morning. The day's task was to wash the wall clean and give it a base layer of paint. The height of the mural was about twelve feet. We were about the same age, but I volunteered to get on the ladder and scrub out the dirt and cobwebs at the top part of the wall. I was just ten minutes into it before someone started to ping my phone with a series of texts. I saw a bunch of pictures Bruce sent me of what looked like pieces of very official paper. "I'm being evicted," he texted. "The sheriff showed up this morning," read another text. "They gave me five days!" I kept on working because I didn't know what to do. Did he even want me to do anything? He had said he hated asking for help. Typical male. But getting kicked out of your home was an extreme circumstance. Still, I didn't think he wanted me to help him. He knew that I was in no position to, anyway. Our relationship was based on not having this kind of expectation of each other. We both wanted that. But why send all these photos to me?

At lunch, I called Bruce back from my car. He picked up right away. "I'm freaking out here," he said. "I don't even know what to think."

"Tell me what happened."

Bruce told me how the sheriff's officers showed up at eight to serve him the papers that he had texted me page by page. "How am I supposed to move and find a place in five days? It's not like I didn't want to pay rent. I'm not a freeloader. They told me I didn't have to. I haven't paid since last March. I can pay some of the back rent." There was an eviction moratorium throughout most of the pandemic. I had heard it was lifted, or some city council people were trying to extend it. But that was the city of LA. Bruce lived in Norwalk. I didn't know what their rules were.

"Today was Wednesday," I said.

"I will be locked out by Monday," he said. "Do they count the weekend? I'm so confused. Can they kick people out? Aren't we still in the middle of a pandemic? And I'm on medical leave."

I mostly just let him speak. I was on the phone with him for about ten minutes when he kept saying more and more, "I'm freaking out. What am I supposed to do?"

Finally, I said, "I'm sure there are others in the same boat. There must be some help out there for tenants. Let me talk to some people."

After we hung up, I called my friend Essie, the one I had been renting a room from. Essie worked for the mayor's office. Housing wasn't her thing, but she must know places where Bruce could find help. She picked up right away. I told her what Bruce was going through. I described him as a friend. She asked me to forward her the pictures he sent me. She didn't hesitate even though I had never mentioned Bruce to her. A few minutes later, she called back.

"Your friend got what's called an unlawful detainer complaint. That just means that his landlord went to court to file an eviction notice. He's not getting kicked out yet, but he does have to file a response to the complaint in court in the next five days. He can contest the eviction if he has a valid reason."

"He's on disability. He used to drive buses for Metro," I said.

"He is?"

"Or he's on medical leave."

Essie made a guttural sound. "Which is it? They're not the same thing."

"I don't know."

I could see her forehead crinkling, wondering how well I actually knew this guy.

"Well, in any case," she continued, "I know there is a nonprofit organization that's stationed at the courthouses that helps tenants fill out these forms. They're not lawyers, but they know what to do. I'll text you the link."

I thanked her and hung up. Her text showed up in the next thirty seconds. Neighborhood Legal Services. I looked up their website. Their self-help center closest to Bruce was at the Superior Court in Pasadena. I relayed all that information to Bruce via text and told him to go that afternoon.

That evening I was waiting for Bruce to text me any updates. I wanted to call him, but I didn't want to crowd him. Instead, I showed the girls some of my drawings on my tablet. They were mostly abstract lines at first. Then I showed them how some of them progressed to paintings. What I had kept. What I had changed. What had evolved in spite of me. Jasmine was totally into it, and her younger sisters only listened because she was.

Their parents came back a little early this time, and they spent some time with the twins after dinner. I was sketching on my tablet when Jasmine sidled up to me on the couch. She probably wanted to talk about art some more.

"You skipped one of the paintings, didn't you?"

"What do you mean?"

"There was one line sketch, the before, that didn't have an after."

I did skip one. I could've lied to her and said that the lines never amounted to anything. But I swiped to the Slutty Nipple and gave her my tablet.

I texted Bruce the next two days, always during lunch, to see how he was doing and whether he found help at the court. On Saturday morning, he finally messaged me back. "When are you coming home?" the text read. "I really wanna see u."

At lunch, I responded, "I don't want to distract you. You have a lot going on." In my mind, I thought I could skip the unofficial party tonight and the official ceremony tomorrow and go straight to him after we wrapped up today. No one would miss me. Not my professor. Except maybe Jasmine. I had promised her that we'd work on doing some line drawings together. Essie was also hosting a potluck watch-party for *The Last of Us* at our place tomorrow night that I half-heartedly said I'd make something for.

"It's been a long week. I could use some distractions," he messaged. Then, "It's not like anything is going to happen during the weekend."

He still didn't tell me whether he had gone to the court and filed a response to his landlord's notice. And I didn't want to keep asking. He did sound chipper, so I thought he must have. Or he was too delusional or sex-starved to see his predicament.

I didn't commit. I just told him I'd have to see how I'd feel tomorrow.

The next morning, I went on a shopping spree before the ceremony. As a thank you for letting me stay with them, I bought Jasmine's parents a bottle of my ex's favorite tequila that I had found in that fancy supermarket. Sixty dollars, with tax, of my own money, since it couldn't be covered by food stamps. I also bought a leather-bound journal for Jasmine to sketch in. Another twenty bucks. I wanted to get the twins something, too. I got them some coloring books that came with their own stickers. Less than five dollars each. I hadn't expected to spend so much, but it felt right. I figured I'd make up for it later. Bruce's response to my last wait-and-see text—a crying emoji, followed by one with its tongue sticking out—didn't come until halfway through the ceremony. I left it alone. Afterward, I sat with Jasmine and her family during lunch for half an hour and gave them my gifts before I split. It wasn't quite a French exit, but I hated a drawn-out goodbye.

Before I got home, I went to an Asian market and picked up potato starch noodles and some produce for the meatless japchae I was going to make for Essie's party. A few guests were vegetarians, and I was glad I didn't have to spend extra on good meat, anyway.

It was also healthy: spinach, onions, carrots, two kinds of capsicum for color (red and yellow—since I wasn't using egg either), and three kinds of mushroom (white, oyster, and shiitake—to give it that meat texture). Japchae was about layering of flavors and required a lot of prepping. Essie's compost would be so happy tonight. She'd already made a Moroccan one-pot couscous. She was already enjoying a glass of chardonnay when I was still cutting my carrots into matchsticks.

"How's your friend doing? The one being evicted? What's his name?" she asked.

"Bruce."

She asked her question again when I was too concentrated on not slicing my fingers. Without looking at her, I said, "I think he's okay. No news is good news, I suppose." We went back to being silent for a while. Her Spotify was playing a SZA song that she liked. When that song ended, I told her the truth, that Bruce was someone I had hooked up with for the last six months. And that the last time, we had dropped E. I had promised Essie years ago, when I became sober, that I would tell her if I was using again. She took a long sip at her wine. I went back to chopping.

Then she said, "I'm worried about you."

"There's nothing to worry about. It's just E, Essie. It barely counts." I wanted to tell her that I didn't feel powerless about my life like before. In fact, it was quite the opposite.

"Not that. You had a stable relationship and now you're hooking up with guys on the verge of eviction?"

"That's not his fault. You're not being fair."

"I love you. You know that. But it's been more than a year. Have you figured out what you want to do? It just feels like you're drifting. What's your next step?"

When one of our friends asked me the same question later that evening, paper plate in his hand, full of the food that I had made, I told him I should be hearing from a few MFA programs I had applied to. He said, "oh." I thought I wasn't being clear. So I listed my top choices and explained why. He just nodded. I was thinking back to my conversation with Essie before the party. She knew all this. She had seen me agonizing over my portfolio as part of my application. Yet, she still asked me about my next step. An MFA, I was reminded again, was not supposed to be a next step, especially at my age.

Quynh, Essie's girlfriend, told me she had lunch with my ex. She reported that my ex had changed jobs. I told her I was glad. He had hated his last job. The morons he used to work for were all he could ever talk about when we talked at the end of each day. When I advised him to look for another job, he told me it wasn't that easy. This friend shook her head. Quynh said his new job paid a lot more but was much worse. Combat pay. That broke my heart.

I surveyed the room of forty- and fifty-somethings. My peers, who were all ostensibly doing better than me. Models of stability and longevity. Couple by couple, I listed their problems in my head: this couple couldn't stop talking about their home improvement that cost them a second mortgage; this woman complained about her husband never getting their children to school on time because it was all she allowed herself to complain about since she had forgiven him about his affair; this couple had stopped having sex after four years; this couple's adopted child resented them for sending him to Chinese school when he was Salvadoran, despite a lifetime of privilege they conferred on him; this couple had an open marriage but only one was taking advantage of it; this woman had a stroke because of the stress of being the sole breadwinner when her wife had seemed to lose all will to work but she was too afraid to divorce her because she would lose half of her possessions; this man crashed his car on his commute home but his lover didn't want to talk about his addiction. All of these people, at the height of their careers, were in golden handcuffs.

I should be the one asking them, "What's your next step?"

Why was I so afraid to be with Bruce and all his mess that he never asked me to be a part of? Why did I make up this arbitrary one-month rule? Why couldn't I live in the glorious present with him? What vestige of my old life was I clinging to? I made Bruce count the days in a month. Hell, he might not even have a home come Monday.

All around the room I saw commitment. They all had once been in love, fire ablaze, but they now settled for embers. I had no doubt that I could be as comfortable as them had I stayed with my ex. But I didn't want commitment.

I wanted presence.

When the TV show began, I went to the kitchen. I packed the unfinished japchae in a Tupperware and took off.

5.

Bruce greeted me, "I'm really glad you came."

On tiptoe, I held his face and kissed him deeply. He pulled me inside. Not wanting to let him go, not wanting to drag my toes, I climbed onto him, my legs around his waist, as he backed through the kitchen, to the living room, and fell onto his couch. I was glad he was home. I had messaged him before I got on the freeway. I told myself to turn back if he didn't return my text by the time I exited the freeway. But I kept going, anyway.

After a few minutes, we took a kissing break. I said, "I didn't know if you were going to be here. You didn't return my text."

"I didn't see it until a few minutes ago. I've been working on a letter to my county supervisor. I wasn't looking at the phone."

I looked at the room. It was more sparse than the last week I was there. The side table was gone, and he took down a mirror from the wall.

"Are you expecting them to come tomorrow?" I asked.

"No. Thanks to you, I filed the paperwork to contest the eviction. I don't know if it would work—these things are so complicated—but it should hold them off for at least a few weeks. I also told my landlord I could pay him some of the back rent. He hasn't responded yet." He slipped his hand underneath my shirt and slowly inched his way to my nipples. "You're my present for a productive week."

"You have my presence."

"What?"

"Oh, I almost forgot. I have a real present for you. Did you eat yet?" Still straddling him, I bent to the floor to reach the tote bag I had dropped in the middle of making out. I took out the japchae.

"You made this? For me?" He actually got a little teary-eyed, like no one else had ever cooked for him before. I didn't have the heart to tell him I made a whole batch for a dozen people who wouldn't miss it. He opened it and saw the ribbons of bright vegetables mixed in with the noodles glistened with sesame oil. "It looks so pretty. It smells so good." Then he looked at me. "I don't know what I've done to deserve this."

"I like being with you, when I'm with you."

"Yeah, two weekends in a row. My spell is working."

While Bruce was eating, I looked over his email to the county supervisor. I told him that the email was too long, that he had included too many details. I suggested keeping the mention of him having been a bus driver for Metro (i.e., he was a public servant), but they didn't have to know that no one ever told him the moratorium was lifted. I sat on his lap while he dictated to me his edits between bites. I told him he didn't have to bad-mouth his landlord. He had a hard time letting that one go. I said the main objective was to get a meeting with the supervisor's staff so they could connect them to county resources. He finally let me delete those five sentences about his landlord. He consoled himself that his landlord might agree to the extended payment plan he offered. I had the feeling that his landlord was just stringing Bruce along without the intention of letting him stay under any circumstances. He probably could make a lot more money with a new tenant.

I trimmed it to half its original length. "Press send?" I asked.

"Press send."

It had taken me a while to understand that, when my ex complained about how much he hated his job, he didn't want me to encourage him to find something better. He didn't need me to tell him that, with his skills and experience in this job market, if he had snapped his fingers and let people know he was available, the job offers would swarm in. He had no intention of changing his station. In fact, he had considered it a "mark of maturity" to weather these hardships. To imagine another career, to pursue the passions of yesteryear—at this age, that was downright childish. When we couldn't let each other be, we had to let it end.

I had some hard truths for Bruce, too. I thought his eviction was inevitable, no matter how good his offer was to pay back the rent he owed, no matter how eloquent the letter to his county supervisor was. But when he wanted to celebrate that milestone of pressing send by going out, I didn't object.

"Like on a date?" I teased him. I could do that because neither of us had to be responsible for the future of the other. All we had was this moment, and it was much easier to make one moment as good as it could get than a lifetime.

He grabbed my hand and kissed the back of it. "I know a bar not too far from here. It's kind of a dive bar."

"Straight?"

"Uber-straight. We have to control ourselves and actually have a conversation."

"We have plenty of conversations."

He winked at me. "Not before sex, though."

The bar called Anarchy was a dive, like he promised. They were playing what sounded like a Spanish rock song from the 1990s. Bruce ordered us each a Jameson with a Bud Light chaser. The bartender, a woman in her fifties with dirty blonde hair piled on top and a leopard tattoo on her upper arm, seemed to know Bruce at least by his face. He refused to let me pay. We did have a good conversation, even if we had to scream into each other's ear. I told him about my week in Santa Paula, staying with Jasmine and her family, and showed him the completed mural on my phone. He told me that in his twenties he had spent a summer thinning peach trees in the San Joaquin Valley. He continued the story but the music got too loud and I caught only every second or third word he said. I gathered he'd worked at that job for just a couple of months, long enough to learn some conversational Spanish, before he quit and moved on. Even Daddy couldn't hack farm work—that was the conclusion. I did enjoy having him breathing in my ear.

By 10 p.m., the bar was getting crowded even though it was a Sunday night and the music had switched to American progressive rock. We were on our second beer and found some open space in the back. Bruce was mouthing the lyrics to some song but he didn't remember the band.

"Everclear," I supplied. Something about him singing to "Father of Mine" was a little bit too on the nose.

He smiled and looked like he was about to kiss me. Instead, he said, "I've never met anyone like you."

Maybe it was the alcohol, but I had the immense urge to touch him. Nothing racy. Hooking his finger would've been enough. I didn't do that. I went to the restroom instead. Someone was at the urinal, so I took the one and only stall to pee. Not that I needed it, but the lone toilet had no seat.

When I came out of the restroom, I couldn't find Bruce. The place was packed. I went to the front and sneaked my head out the door for a look outside. There was a queue of about a dozen people, half of them eyeing me.

The bouncer said, "You're in or you're out. If you go out, you'll have to get back in line."

Just then I spotted Bruce half a block down. His phone lit up his face.

"I guess I'm out," I told the bouncer.

When Bruce saw me walking toward him, he smiled. He said, "I was going to text you. It was too loud in there to take the call."

"Is everything okay?"

"Yeah. I have to run an errand. Do you want to come with?"

I nodded. It wasn't like I had a choice. He didn't answer me when I asked what it was about until we were back in his truck.

"It's Damian." He had just started the ignition. I thought I had misheard him.

"The tweaker?"

"Yes."

"What does he want?"

"He had a date tonight. I dropped him off earlier. I guess it didn't work out. I'm just going to pick him up."

I was silent. I was processing. I was trying to think of what to say.

Bruce continued, "He's been couch-surfing at my place the last couple of nights. He was going to be gone all night at this date, and we'd have the place to ourselves." That was why he hadn't told me until now. "Knowing him, it won't take him long to find someone else online."

"So, what? You're just going to chauffeur him to the next party?"

"It'll just be a brief interruption of our date." He winked at me. It was both cute and annoying.

"Do you think you should be letting him stay with you?"

"I don't trust him. When he's there, I keep my valuables locked up. Not that I have that many valuables nowadays."

"You're on the verge of getting kicked out. I can't see how that helps you. And he seems like the kind of guy who can find help easily." I wanted to remind Bruce about how he was able to find people to help him move before (a place he apparently had lost in a matter of months) when Bruce had set some boundaries. I didn't because Bruce's face had lost all humor.

"Look, I was Damian when I was his age. I know what that's like. I was lucky to have some people look out for me. He's reckless, I know. I just don't want him to end up dead in the street. So yes, as long as I have a place where he can stay and be safe, even for a night, I'll help."

"It's not your job to save him," I said.

"Who says anything about saving anybody?" He sucked in his breath.

I was getting worked up, too, and I was trying to figure out why. I didn't think it was jealousy. It had nothing to do with our "date." "Let's not talk about it anymore," I said. He had made up his mind about picking Damian up, anyway. *Father gave him a name and walked away*, just like the song said. And now Bruce thought he needed to be a Daddy taking care of everyone to be loved. *He will always be safe. He will always be lame.* Too on the nose, like a fist punch.

A few seconds later, he muttered, "You don't know me." It wasn't mean. It was almost halfway between an accusation and a regret. I just let it slide.

Typical Male didn't use his GPS and insisted that he knew where he was going. We cruised to one of those shoreline high-rises in Long Beach, where he had dropped Damian off earlier that night. Bruce was sure he had the right place, but the young man was nowhere to be found. I looked out the window and up. The fog had rolled in and anything above the fifth floor of the building was lost in it. The lights from some of the units shone weakly, and I wondered what had happened to Damian's date. Did the twink get a little too bossy and overstay his welcome, or was the sugar daddy too old and fat even for a tweaker? Maybe he had no use for Damian other than a cum dump. I wished it was the latter, that he was the one who was put out.

Bruce called him on his phone, and Damian answered right away. He was a couple of intersections north of us, closer to downtown. Just like he said he would be in his voicemail. I could hear him on Bruce's Bluetooth in the truck. He sounded impatient, and I felt a little sorry for Bruce. Someone was always being used by someone else. I punched in the intersection on my phone's GPS and held it in front of him until we got there.

Damian got into the back seat in the cab, right behind me. Bruce introduced us, and Damian popped his head between Bruce and me and gave me an enthusiastic "hey" that I couldn't muster in return. "What happened, man?" Bruce asked.

"It just wasn't happening," he said. That was all he would volunteer.

As Bruce started driving away, he said, "Dude, kinda on a date here." Bruce smiled at the both of us, not so much to defuse the situation, but frankly a little proudly like he was showing me off. If I weren't so middle-aged, I'd probably blush.

"I'm sorry. I'll get out of your hair."

"Maybe you can text the guy you saw a couple of nights ago."

"On it. That's not a bad idea."

I could tell Bruce was waiting for me to give my approval, but I just refused to look at him. So he grabbed my hand. I turned around just enough to see Damian for the first time. He wasn't as skinny as I had imagined. His blond hair was definitely not his natural color. He was typing on his phone and then he looked up at me. He didn't seem very high.

I asked, "Have you eaten yet?" Fuck, did I turn into my mother? He caught me off-guard.

He said he was fine and went back to his phone. The light made his face paler.

Occasionally I heard a couple of different sound effects coming from the back, as if he was toggling between apps. I took that to mean he was working on his next trick. I kept quiet. Each sound, as faint as it might be, a step closer to alone time with Bruce.

"What I really want, though," Damian announced, as we got within a mile of Bruce's, "is to take a shower and just crash on your couch."

Bruce showed no reaction on his face. It certainly wasn't a yes, but what was I supposed to say?

Bruce went to his room to continue taking it apart. When Damian went into the bathroom, Bruce took one empty nightstand into the kitchen and started sorting the junk in the second one. His guitar was in the kitchen, too. I didn't know if that was with the stuff that he was giving away. When I heard the showers, I went to Bruce in the bedroom.

"Is he staying, or is he going?"

Bruce shrugged without looking at me. "He always finds someone."

I thought to myself, *And tonight that chump is you.* I didn't want to distract him from packing, and he didn't seem like he wanted to talk about it. So I went back to the living room. I thought maybe if I could just occupy the couch, Damian's bed, long enough, he would get the hint and leave. I finally returned Essie's many texts and told her I was okay. I almost told her that I wouldn't be home tonight, but I wasn't convinced of it myself. Plus, it was already midnight. The party must have been over for at least an hour and she was probably in bed with Quynh, anyway. Tomorrow was Monday.

Damian finally came out of the bathroom. In his pajamas. He flopped on the other end of the couch, butt first, as if he had done it every night. He was on the phone, but just scrolling this time, not DMing anyone. He didn't seem like he had anywhere to go.

I had made a choice to get away from my friends and come here. Nothing had been my choice since then. Now I had one: should *I* stay or should I go? When Damian started playing some TikTok videos on his phone, the choice seemed clear.

I went into Bruce's room. Squatting next to his bed, he peered over a box he had retrieved from underneath it. He turned around and smiled at me.

"Hey, stranger." He got up and sat on the bed. He patted the empty space next to him, beckoning me. I wanted so much to stand between his legs and have him catch me as I collapsed onto him. But I only reached for his hand.

"I think I'm going to go."

"Why?"

"I don't want to make you choose." Because he wouldn't choose me. He needed to feel needed. And I didn't need him.

He sighed heavily and looked away, but he kept my hand in his. I had to remind myself to be strong.

He turned back to me and said, "Let me at least walk you out."

My heart sank.

I passed the living room, with Bruce in tow, without saying goodbye to Damian. Going through the kitchen was like Orpheus ascending from hell; I didn't dare to look back, and someone would disappear at the end of this trek. All of a sudden, I heard a loud thud. I turned and found the coffee machine fallen in the kitchen sink, the pot now shattered in shards.

"Bruce!"

"I'm trying to make everyone happy," he said. Then he rushed past me and out of the apartment.

Outside, he waited for me by my car.

"I know why you're leaving. I'm no good for you," he said.

"Is that what you think? That's not why I'm leaving."

"I'm not. I'm too messy for you."

We stood silent for a long time. Neither one of us made a move.

He finally said, "I'm not going to ask you to stay."

"I can't go if you think I'm leaving because you're not good for me." When he didn't say anything, I added, "I'm not afraid of your mess."

"Your action says something different."

"Bruce."

His eyes were wet. "You want to go. Go."

"I can't go like this."

He smiled and gave me a brief kiss on the mouth. "Go. Text me when you get home."

He disappeared behind the gates before I could stop him.

I was flying through the 5 after midnight. Part of me wanted to get home as quickly as possible. The rest of me wanted to slow down, in case I changed my mind or in case he called. I just left an angry and horny Daddy with a guy less than half my age and more than twice as cute who was possibly high and would fuck anything. How long did I have to power down before a reset?

The house was dark when I came home. I quietly went to my room and thought about texting Bruce like he'd asked. But then I thought better of it. My mind was already a jumble of insecurities. What if he didn't text me right back? I would never fall asleep. And I wanted to sleep. I wanted this day to end.

I took a gummy and found some dream music on a Spotify channel, the forest noises low and eerie.

At some point in the night, I woke up to pee. The room was still dark. After I came back from the bathroom, I checked the phone. It was almost five. I was still groggy from the gummy, but feeling rested and surprisingly calm. Bruce had texted me, after 1 a.m., and asked me if I was home yet.

I messaged him, "I was home. Went straight to bed."

I climbed back under the blanket and curled up. I was relieved. Monday I could sleep in late, do some painting at home, before going to my night class. And somehow his text made me think my worst fear didn't happen.

6.

Essie was gone by the time I woke up the second time. I took a long shower and then ate the leftovers from the party I found in the fridge: a fried chicken breast, some couscous, and the last of an overdressed kale salad. I didn't even bother nuking the chicken. I watched the finale that I had missed last night, glancing at my phone every five minutes. After that, I moved a few chairs back to the kitchen where they belonged and took out the trash. I gathered that the party had ended later than usual. It was almost two, after all that dawdling, when I finally got to my painting. Even then, I wasn't into it.

Bruce hadn't texted me back.

So I messaged him, "I'm sorry about last night. It wasn't my place to tell you how to be with your friends."

"Friends" was too generous to describe Damian, but the olive branch was genuine. I just wished I hadn't needed to offer it first.

A notification appeared on my phone, but not the one I had been expecting. One of the three graduate schools I had applied to emailed me to tell me I could log on to see whether I had been accepted. It was starting, and I wasn't ready for it yet. I decided to sketch something new in my notebook instead. After an hour—and no word from Bruce—I left for the studio on campus, even though the class wouldn't begin for another three hours.

I came home around 9 p.m. Essie was on the phone with Quynh. I went straight to my room and signed on to the admission portal on my laptop, finally.

I was not accepted.

They didn't even bother to "regret to inform" anymore.

I grabbed my phone and texted Bruce, "Really? You got nothing for me?" It had been almost twelve hours since the olive branch.

Essie knocked on my door and asked if she could come in. I closed the laptop and said yes. I told myself I had two more chances.

"Hey," she said, standing by the doorway. "You left without saying anything last night."

"I'm sorry."

"It's okay. Did you go to that Bruce guy?"

I nodded.

"I figured as much. I didn't say anything to anyone. I hope it was fun. I didn't hear you come in last night." Before I could decide how to respond to her, she continued, "You missed the big announcement." She smiled impishly.

"What?"

She held up her left hand. There was a ring on her middle finger, a silver band with sapphire blue across in the middle. "Quynh's measurement was off. We have to resize it, but we're engaged." She almost skipped where she stood. I got up to give her a hug. She sat on my bed and pulled me down with her to tell me everything. They didn't want a huge ceremony. Rob and Jae offered to host it at their home; Jae, the alcoholic with the long commute, would even get ordained online to officiate it. It would be a short engagement, probably summer or fall. Essie and Quynh had started dating in 2021, during the pandemic. This was not uncommonly quick as lesbian timelines went. Quynh would give up her condo in Glendale and move in after the wedding.

"But you don't have to move out right away," she assured me. I wasn't even thinking about that, though Essie had said it in a way that made it sound like a natural conclusion. I thought I had just been given notice. "By then, you'll probably be packing for grad school, anyway."

"Fingers crossed," I said. I didn't want to ruin the moment by telling her of my first rejection. Two more chances. Not wanting to think more about it, I gave her another hug. "I'm really happy for you."

"Really?" she said behind my back. "I know you're not big on monogamy these days."

"If that's what makes you happy, Ester Maria Coleman, then happy monogamy is what you shall have."

She hugged me tighter. "Don't worry. I won't ask you to be the best man." That was Essie's politician way of regretfully informing me that she didn't choose me.

Essie stayed in my room for almost forty minutes. Only after she left did I realize that Bruce had texted me back, just a few minutes after I sent mine.

He asked, "Why did it take you more than four hours to get home?"

Then ten minutes later, he parroted me. "You got nothing for me?"

He thought the time I texted him last night, at four in the morning after I relieved myself, was the time I had just gotten home, that I had left his place to hook up with someone else. What could I say? These long minutes of silence, he probably thought I was either guilty or trying to cook up an excuse.

I told the truth. I told him I had to medicate myself to sleep to rid the image of him fucking Damian in my head.

He said Damian had left a couple of hours after me. Someone came and picked him up, and he had not heard from him since. If only I had waited, I could've spared both of us a miserable night. He might have believed that I hadn't gone behind his back, but he was clearly still feeling a lot salty about me leaving him.

I asked him what it was that he wanted of us. He said he had no expectation. That was clearly not the case, though I didn't contradict him then. He shot the question back at me. I told him I just wanted to go back to where we were before, when we climbed onto each other's body each time like it was the first time, new and not new, like déjà vu, that feeling of being exactly where we were supposed to be.

He asked me to come over then. A redo.

"I can't. I'm behind in my school work. You need to focus on not getting evicted."

"Rules." I wasn't sure he meant it in a mocking way, or a contemptuous one.

I asked him if he had heard back from his county supervisor. He didn't reply. That was all for the night.

7.

I didn't hear from Bruce the following week, and I was fine with it. I had helped him probably more than most people in his life. He should know he could call me if he needed anything. The silence was typical between our sexual encounters—he went on with his life and I with mine until we met again—but it didn't feel like the carefree laissez-faire this time. It felt like holding back. Punishment.

Friday during dinner, when we were recapping the week to each other, I told Essie everything.

"This is a fuck buddy?" she asked.

"For the last six months, yes."

"It sounds kinda intense for a fuck buddy. I mean, you were both in tears the last time you left his place."

I knew where she was going with this. "Do I have feelings for him? Yes, but we're not boyfriends." It struck me that we didn't have a word for what Bruce and I had. Essie wasn't wrong: he was more than a fuck buddy. And the more I knew about him, the more intimate our sex was. But after that, we had lives we led independently. I pointed out to Essie that Bruce and I had not spoken or texted in a week, and I felt totally fine.

"And you haven't seen other people in the last six months? It sounds monogamous."

"Only because polyamory is so much work, especially for introverts," I countered. "This is exhausting enough. I can't imagine another Bruce."

Essie said "okay" like she didn't want to argue with me.

"It's not a relationship," I said.

"I sure hope not. He's not very stable."

"Well, neither am I. If we were in a relationship, things about him that I could ignore would start bugging me, and vice versa. We would want to change each other. We lead independent lives. We take care of our own shit." I didn't catch myself quick enough before I added, "We don't have any expectations of each other."

It was what he had said, unconvincingly. Essie looked at me with the same dubiousness I had.

Maybe Bruce and I had passed our sweet spot. Maybe that was why I was afraid to call him now.

Another week and nothing from Bruce. As much as he detested my rules, he followed them and it was not a surprise that he would leave me alone for almost a month before scheduling our next hookup. Our last date broke so many rules, and it ended disastrously. Maybe he wanted to take his foot off the pedal, too. Or maybe he was still sore. Abandonment issue wasn't a small thing with him.

On the other hand, I got my second rejection. This time from Cal State LA. Right in my backyard.

When I told Essie, she said, "That was your safety school, anyway. You still have your top choices."

Choice. Singular. I still hadn't told her about the first rejection.

When I finally shared the overdue bad news with her, she put her hand on mine and said, "Hey, even if you don't get into the last school, you have tried. You can always tell yourself that. Maybe that's a blessing in disguise. You've tried the unbeaten path and you can go back to the original programming."

Years ago, when we were college students, we would play a drinking game where someone had to drink when they committed a literary faux pas, like a mixed metaphor, like she had just now. We were such grammar nerds. I broke away from Essie's hold and reached for my glass of wine. Without looking at her, I threw my head back with what was left in that glass.

He was incommunicado for another two weeks. He didn't return my text, even on the exact day of the one month since the last time we had sex, or a week later, a month after we last saw each other, the night of our first and only fight. He was usually the one who reminded me of the imminent end of our moratorium, my moratorium. This wasn't him being mad at me. Something was wrong, I could tell.

That night, I drove down to Downey. By the time I parked outside of his apartment, the street on a Saturday night was suburban dark. I passed his neighbor's front unit, where the light from the TV from the inside created a corona effect around the shuttered window. The stereo sound was a perfect cover for my trespass. I jogged up the stairs quickly and lightly to Bruce's place.

The vertical blinds over his kitchen window hung in parallel. My heart sank at the emptiness inside. I shone the flashlight from my phone into the window, as if I were expecting the old appliances would reappear like invisible ink.

I moved to the door. It was ajar. More accurately, it couldn't close right. It had been broken into. If Bruce was evicted, the sheriff wasn't supposed to force their way in like that. Did he resist? Or did he break into his own home later to retrieve what he didn't have time to gather? (Maybe his guitar?) Neither was good.

A refrigerator still hummed. But I was afraid to turn on the lights. In the dark I still found my way to the living room easily. Moonlight poured through the window on that other side of the apartment. I could tell the original color of the carpeting from where Bruce's couch used to be. The couch where I'd last sat, should-I-stay-or-should-I-go wading in my mind. The couch where he'd played his guitar, composing a song about strawberries and nipples. Dirt surrounded where it used to be like a chalk outline.

He was gone.

8.

Days later, I finally told Essie about my reconnaissance. She said, not in a callous way, "I'm sure you haven't heard the last of him."

I said, "I think you're right. That cat has nine lives. He's a survivor." When I heard myself say that, I imagined it was the same Bruce would say about me. And that made me smile, however Essie wanted to interpret that.

"Are you okay?" she asked.

"We were messy. We were bright. We were a supernova."

"I think you might have just romanticized it a little bit," Essie said, in a way that only someone who had known a person for decades could say.

"Maybe," I said. "Probably. But I'm not getting married to it."

9.

In August, Essie and Quynh had a combined bachelorette party. My ex, who had just bought a new house in Palos Verdes on the bluffs over the Pacific, offered to host it. Essie said they could go with someone else. It had been three years since our breakup, and I didn't expect the about-wed to sacrifice an ocean view and the only place in LA where they could have a breezy outdoor party in the afternoon at the height of summer for my sake. From the way they described his new home, I joked, there must be plenty of room for us to avoid each other.

"Is it okay with him?"

"Are you kidding?" she said. "He wants you there. I'm convinced we're just a ruse."

By then everyone knew that I wasn't going to grad school in the fall. The last rejection had come as unceremoniously as the first two. Strangely, at the party, no one asked me what my next step was. Most of them just avoided me altogether. Too bad, I had really wanted to throw my uncertain future in their faces and see what they would say. I had an idea of turning their advices and platitudes into a new series of paintings and calling it "Daddy Issues."

My ex brought out a giant heart-shaped cake with red and pink ruffled icing all over the top that made it look like a vagina. As a couple dozen people ogled over it, he sat with me and asked if I had found a new place for after Essie and Quynh got married. That was less than two months away.

"I have a couple of leads," I said. "A couple of my classmates from last semester need to find new roommates in the fall."

He just nodded and looked away, to the vast horizon ahead of us. It was past seven, but the summer sun was relentless, like it was never going to disappear. He was trying, and I loved him for it.

"Don't worry," I added. "I'll be fine. It'd be like an artist colony."

He nodded again, but this time, he looked straight at me. "I miss you."

I couldn't tell him the same. So I asked him, "Are you happy?"

He chuckled loud and said, "It's such a *you* thing to ask." I thought we were going to have a fight because it should be the only one constant question that anyone would ask of themselves and each other. But then he said, "Not as happy as them." His head indicated our friends, who were striking a pose with the cake. Essie was acting shocked by it, while Quynh stuck out her tongue, miming cunnilingus. A silly picture.

I laughed. "Fake oral sex is not happiness."

"You know what I mean."

"And you know what I mean." I regretted saying that. In the old days, those would be fighting words. But my ex just put his hand on mine. "Would you stay the night?" He was really trying. When I didn't say no, he said, "You could hear the waves in my bedroom. That, plus being next to you, will make me happy."

I could feel Essie's eyes on us, on his hand on mine.

"If I stay, it would just be for tonight."

He squeezed my hand harder.

I grinded him until he cried. We hadn't had sex like that since perhaps the third year of our relationship. My ex was right about the waves. They kept crashing after we were done.

He was up before I was in the morning. I found him in the kitchen, dressed in his polo and slacks, reading his Sunday papers. When he saw me, he got up from the table and said, "I could make you an espresso." I pulled out the Calendar section but I watched him instead of reading it.

Sunday papers had been our routine for a while, too.

"You're all dressed. Are you heading out?" I asked.

"Yeah, to my office. I usually work Saturday, but I didn't yesterday because of the party. I need to get ahead of the week. You can hang out here if you want." The machine started hissing. "Would you like a latte?" he said. "I'm no artist, but I've been working on some primitive foam art."

I said, "Is that the same espresso machine in their registry? What other fancy ideas did you give them?"

"We can go in together for a gift." He looked at me playfully, and then added, "if you want."

I could feel it coming. He pulled out some milk from his refrigerator, whose doors looked like the rest of the cabinetry. He steamed up the milk in his machine. "I've been thinking."

And there it was.

"What if you just move in here after they get married? Not like moving in together, moving in together. Not like before. You'd get your own room." He seemed concentrated on the latte. From behind, I could pretend he was talking to someone else. "God knows I got plenty of rooms in this house." I was about to say his name to make him stop, but he put his masterpiece in front of me and continued. "Try it on for a year. I make enough money for the both of us. You can try applying for grad school again. We can turn one of the rooms into a studio."

The old him would've considered grad school at my age frivolous. He was really trying. I wanted to say yes.

"Swap out the Slutty Nipple in your portfolio with something new. I'm sure you'll have something better by the time you apply again." If he had tried this hard three years ago, we might have stayed together. But then I would still be miserable.

I thought about my father, who had to give up his teaching vocation to roam unfamiliar streets day in, day out to put food on our table, until he retired at sixty-nine with a bad back and a slow heart. He got three mediocre years before he passed. I looked at my ex's dining table in the next room, which could hold a buffet large enough for a small village. But he wasn't so different from my father. *Am I really thinking about going back*, I thought. *Bitch, I'm the one with the daddy issue.*

I said, "What if I asked you if we could get together once a month, just like last night? Then we go away and we do our own thing. What would you say to that?"

He looked blankly at me. "I wish I could be that for you."

I began to cry softly. Even with all the riches surrounding him, he reminded me, even more in this moment, of my dad, an immigrant who had deferred his happiness. My ex had waited, held on for me. He had not moved forward. And I was not faultless. "I'm sorry for making you feel bad for wanting someone who I'm not." I buried my face in my hands.

He said, "You're still becoming."

It was, in the way that he said it, strange and unexpected: not meaning incomplete or immature. It was apt. My hands clasped his, replacing my face. I looked up at him. "I am sorry, but I'm not sorry about last night."

He kissed the top of my head. I looked down at my uneven latte. A tempest. A swirling pattern around a white tip like a snow-capped hill. It was perfect.

IN THE ZERO STREET FICTION SERIES

All Daughters Are Awesome Everywhere: Stories
by DeMisty D. Bellinger

I Make Envy on Your Disco
by Eric Schnall

Daddy Issues: Stories
by Eric C. Wat

Forget I Told You This
by Hilary Zaid

www.ingramcontent.com/pod-product-compliance
Lightning Source LLC
Chambersburg PA
CBHW020828110725
29381CB00006B/6
* 9 7 8 1 4 9 6 2 4 3 5 8 4 *